DEATH
FORCE

"I am extremely sorry, Adam Steele. I had hoped to convince you with the facts that we deserve to succeed in our aim. Force is our last resort."

Steele was aware of blood in his mouth and running out over his lower lip. The whole area of his shoulders and neck where the man gripped him was numb. His belly was on fire. He could not feel the floor beneath his feet. Another right cross slammed into his jaw and a tooth punctured flesh again to spurt fresh blood against his palate.

Steele struggled to detach his mind from his physical being: tried to drag it out of the sea of pain to search for a reason to explain the group's new tactic. For it made no sense at all. But perhaps there was no sense to it. Maybe desperation had driven them to this extreme of spite, pure and simple. . . .

THE ADAM STEELE SERIES:

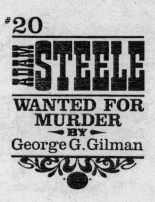

#20

ADAM STEELE

WANTED FOR MURDER

BY

George G. Gilman

PINNACLE BOOKS   NEW YORK

STEELE #20: WANTED FOR MURDER

Copyright © 1979 by George G. Gilman

A Pinnacle Book, published by arrangement with New English Library Limited.

First printing, January 1982

ISBN: 0-523-41453-6

Cover illustration by George Bush

Printed in the United States of America

PINNACLE BOOKS, INC.
1430 Broadway
New York, New York 10018

For
Jane
quite simply, with love.

WANTED FOR MURDER

Chapter One

THE MAN picked up the Colt Hartford rifle from where it leaned against the wall in a corner of the dirty, ill-furnished hotel room and glanced down at the gold plate screwed to the right-hand side of the fire-charred rosewood stock. The inscription engraved on the plate read: TO BENJAMIN P. STEELE, WITH GRATITUDE—ABRAHAM LINCOLN.

But Adam Steele did not have to remind himself of how a long-dead president of the United States had expressed his appreciation to an ally who died on that same April night in 1865. For the rifle—the only material possession Adam Steele had inherited from his murdered father—had over the years become like an extension of the hands in which he carried it now to the

1

greased and smudged window of the small room.

Outside, across the *Embarcadero* and the piers and ferry slips, the surface of San Francisco Bay was serenely smooth except where the water was broken and made briefly white by the bow waves and wakes of boats that moved lazily toward and away from the city: making best use of the warm breezes that blew through the fading light of evening.

He stood at the window for several minutes, as the crimson sun dipped from sight far out over the Pacific Ocean and the lights came on in the city built upon many hills: a frown of deep, soured thought fixed to his freshly shaved face.

It was neither a handsome nor an ugly face: comprised of features that revealed nothing of the character of the man behind them—except sometimes when he was only minutes or seconds away from killing a man. The features were regular, their structure lean. The eyes were coal black, the mouth line gentle and the jaw faintly jutting. The skin which was stretched taut over the sparse flesh across the unprominent bones was deeply tanned and scored with countless cracks—many more than was usual for a man in his late thirties. Also contributing to the impression that he was older was the prematurely gray hair which he kept clipped short, except where it grew bushy in long sideburns. Only here and there did a trace of the former auburn show.

His build was also lean, but the flesh was hard and muscular and anyone who gave Steele a second glance was likely to realize that he was stronger than most men who stood little more than five and a half feet tall.

As he watched day turn into night from the second-story window of the Havelock Hotel he was dressed like a man all set to venture out in search of the best pleasures that San Francisco could offer. His well-tailored suit was pale blue, with beneath it a purple vest and lace-trimmed white shirt, a black bootlace tie knotted neatly at the apex of the collar. On his head was a wide-brimmed, low-crowned black Stetson with a thick, sheened leather band. The riding boots, which he wore inside the cuffs of his pants, were also black, polished to a deep shine.

At odds with the brand-new clothes was a pair of black buckskin gloves fitted skin-tight to his hands. These were scuffed, stained, and torn from many years of hard wear. The split in the seam on the outside right leg of his pants, from knee to lower calf, was recently done: carefully stitched at top and bottom to prevent its enlarging.

He looked like a rich dandy, totally out of context in the dollar-a-night waterfront hotel. Which is exactly what he would have been had the cards continued to be good to him. But at the poker game which had ended in the chilly early morning he had been left with ten cents.

These coins rattled against each other now in his pants pocket as he turned away from the window and moved across the cramped, roach-infested room to the door. The frown was gone from his face before he stepped out into the hallway, his features showing nothing of the remnants of self-anger. He canted the Colt Hartford to his left shoulder and clutched the frame of the rifle with knuckle-straining tightness: the only sign that there never really had been a decision to be made. No matter how dire his circumstances he would never sell his father's gun—nor even try to raise some money on the intrinsic value of the engraved gold stock plate.

There were no lamps in the windowless hallway but the yellow light of many kerosene lamps reached down into the darkness from the balcony above the hotel's Bay City bar and gambling hall. Although it was still only early evening, a barrage of noise also carried, subdued by distance, to the far end of the hallway. The level of sounds—talk, laughter, a fiddle and piano, the rattle of coins and the clinks of bottle necks against glasses—rose as the dudishly attired Steele advanced upon its source. So that soon he could not hear the creak of bedsprings, lustful groans of men and the squeals of pretended enjoyment of women which sounded in some of the rooms to either side of him.

4

The balcony was twice as wide as the hall-way, with the doors to more rooms on the right and a waist-high balustrade on the other side which made a right-angle turn at the far end to become the stairway banister. For a few moments Steele stood at the rail, peering down through a layer of aromatic tobacco smoke at the crowded scene below.

It was a big room, plusher than the upstairs accommodation. A bar with a polished wooden top ran along the rear wall under the balcony, tended by six fast-working barmen. Tables for drinking and the preliminaries of whoring were grouped at one end of the place while at the other were those for cards and games of chance. Between the two was an open area with a circular stage at the center. On this stage the piano player and the man with the fiddle provided music for men who could only afford dance tickets after buying straight liquor for themselves and colored-water cocktails for the overpainted partners of their choice.

The dancing area was polished boarding. There was sawdust to absorb the spilled liquor, beer, and spit on the floor where the drinking was done. The gamblers had the benefit of carpet. Oil paintings in gilt frames hung around the whitewashed plastered walls and there was a long, high mirror in back of the glass and bottle-lined shelves behind the bar.

Through the blue haze of smoke and in the artificial light of the dozen kerosene lamps hung from the ceiling, chandelier fashion in two groups, the place looked at its best for the seamen, land-bound drifters, and local city dwellers who patronized it. Uncrowded in the early morning, the cracks and the dirt and the stains of age and ill-use showed up.

For almost two weeks Adam Steele had seen the place at its best and worst as he gambled through the nights at a poker table. Betting the value of his hands, ignoring alcohol to drink coffee, and devoting all his attention to the cards and the other players to the total exclusion of the whores of many nationalities who plied their trade around him. At first whenever his fortunes rose the obese Madam Mary urged her youngest and prettiest girls to flout the promise of their high-priced favors close to the table where he played. While her skinny husband who was the owner of the Havelock Hotel tried to press a complimentary bottle of imported champagne on him and rent him the best and most expensive room in the place.

But after he had politely declined all offers they left him alone: except with their tongues—resentfully accusing him of being a milksop homosexual when he spent most of a night's winnings on fancy clothes and relishing his ill luck when he had to sell his horse, saddle, and bedroll to pay for three aces which had looked good until another man showed his four eights. But none of the talk was pitched above the level of whispers, for despite Steele's subdued, almost reticent manner, there was the ever-present Colt Hartford revolving rifle to consider. Which, together with the well-worn black gloves and the darker eyes that never showed a flicker of warmth, suggested this was a man best left alone if that was how he chose it to be.

He moved away from the rail and started along the balcony toward the head of the stairs, lips pursed and eyes impassive as he experienced mild regret at the financial necessity of having to leave the Havelock Hotel. It was not the best San Francisco had to offer but neither was it the worst. And it served its purpose for men such as Adam Steele. In its smoke-laden atmosphere beneath the flattering lamplight surrounded by the sounds of people enjoying themselves, a man with a few dollars in his pocket could believe he was sampling a taste of the good life. Even a man who had once been privileged to have the best of everything.

Then Steele came to an abrupt halt, his head swinging to rake his eyes away from the scene below to fix their implaccable stare on a wrenched open door.

A woman screamed in terror, the sound filling the balcony but becoming lost as it fell into the clamor of noise from the saloon.

"Come back here you stinkin' bitch!" a man snarled.

The open doorway was twenty feet ahead of where Steele had halted. He started forward again, unconcerned by the fear and anger, for disagreements between a woman and a man were nothing unusual in a whorehouse.

But then the woman lunged out of the doorway, naked, wth her long black hair streaming back from her head. He recognized her as one of Madam Mary's prize whores: an eighteen-year-old Chinese named Lotus Blossom. He also recognized the degree of fear which was carved into the smooth-skinned face of the girl—changing her delicate beauty to ugliness.

She had looked first toward the top of the stairs, then snapped her head around. When she saw Steele she skidded to a stumbling halt. Her dark eyes pleaded for help and she stretched out both arms toward him. The scream was curtailed and she worked her lips open and closed: but the words remained trapped in her fear-constricted throat. Her naked flesh rippled in a convulsive spasm of trembling.

Steele lengthened his stride.

Lotus Blossom half turned from the waist to look back into the room from which she had escaped.

A gunshot sounded.

A small dark hole marred the creamy smoothness in the lower slope of the girl's left breast. The impact of the bullet jerked her sideways and she hit the balustrade which caused a spurt of slick crimson to shoot out of the wound. She whimpered and turned, so that her back folded over the rail. The spilling blood coursed down

8

over the slight hump of her belly and started to soak into the black triangle of her pubic hair.

"Adam Steele!" she shrieked, the power of her dying breath driving her voice to the upper limit of shrillness and loudness.

Every other sound in the saloon was abruptly curtailed. Every eye swept to stare up at the balcony. In time to see the corpse of Lotus Blossom slip over the rail and fall twenty feet to crash unfeelingly to the floor in front of the bar.

Screams and curses ripped from throats then. A few people lunged forward to stoop and crouch beside the naked, blood-spattered corpse. Most returned their shocked and angry eyes toward the balcony where Steele was moving again, the rifle cocked and leveled from his left hip.

"You murderin' bastard!"

Steele recognized the voice of Madam Mary but paid no attention to what she shrieked. Until first a single shot and then a fusillade exploded. Wood chips from the balustrade and plaster from the ceiling showered him as he swung to a halt in the doorway.

He smelled perfume, then the saline air off the bay. The window was open and he glimpsed a face there, just above the sill between the white knuckles of two hands. Then the hands and the face were gone, the gray-bearded man releasing his grip to drop out of sight.

The meaning of what was happening behind and below him hit Steele as he plunged into the room and ran between the bed and the bureau to the window. Bullets were still being exploded upward, the gunshots giving impetus to the enraged words vented from countless throats. His name sounded louder than the obscenities.

He reached the window and peered down into the dark alley that ran in back of the hotel. An overturned trash can rolled and rattled. A man, no more than a tall thin shadow, made a sharp turn and disappeared into another alley that ran west toward Steuart Street.

"You won't get away, you swish little punk!" a man roared and again Steele recognized a familiar voice. Rod Stockton, a giant of a man employed at the Havelock Hotel to calm troublemakers.

His warning ended the gunshots and quieted most of the other voices. The stair treads rang under the impact of his footfalls as he took them two at a time.

Steele made a genuine decision now: hurled the rifle out into the alley and went down in its wake, using the same technique as the man with the gray beard. But the fall was still a long one and although he bent his legs the right amount to absorb the impact of landing, it still felt as if every bone in his body came within part of a degree of snapping. There was no time to indulge the pains and he reached for the rifle and powered up from the crouch into a sprint, driven to escape in the wake of the gray-bearded man by the only other two choices open to him—to kill Stockton or himself be killed or wounded by a bullet from the big man's Colt .45.

As he skidded around the corner into the alley leading to Steuart Street, the handgun sent a shot after him, the bullet chipping brick dust from the wall only six inches from his bobbing head. Rod Stockton cursed his anger at having missed.

Steele slowed down and tried to ignore the pain of jarred limbs as he turned north on Steuart and forced his gait to appear casual. Lights glistened on the sweat beads that squeezed from his wide-open pores. His chest rose and fell too fast for the pretense to be effective. But the whore who spoke to him from the darkened porchway of a closed liquor store viewed him only as a man and potential client as he checked the busy street in both directions for a sign of the killer.

"You lookin' for someone like me, mister?"

He stopped and his aching legs welcomed the chance to rest. "Only if you've got a gray beard," he rasped, taking another careful look in both directions along the sidewalks on each side of the street.

"I ain't old enough for that, mister. Black, like on my head."

As she spoke the whore moved forward a

11

pace into the fringe of the moon and lamplight that illuminated the street. Then hiked up her long skirt and petticoats to reveal her bare white legs with a triangle of luxuriant black hair where they met at the base of her bulging belly.

Steele glanced at the obscene display, then at the raddled ugliness of the whore's middle-aged face.

"Three dollars for the time of your life, mister," she offered.

Steele moved away from the whore as he heard shouts in the alley at the side of the liquor store. "Not just the price I'd have trouble raising, ma'am," he drawled.

Chapter Two

HE WAS on the far side of the street and weaving between strollers toward the junction of Market and Sacramento when the tall and broad Rod Stockton came running out of the alley at the head of a group of men carrying guns.

Although his slight build and nondescript features normally allowed him to get easily lost in a crowd, tonight in San Francisco was an exception. For he was just back of the waterfront on the southeast fringe of the city's sailortown section, finely dressed in clothing that marked him out among the other men and their women who thronged the street.

Even so, only the unaccompanied whores would have taken any notice of him had not one of their number felt resentment toward him.

For a long time he forced himself to maintain a casual gait, moving marginally faster than the evening strollers around him. More difficult to resist was the urge to look back over his shoulder and across the street. And when he did chance such a backward glance he was in time to see the ugly-faced whore step from the porch of the liquor store and raise an arm to point at him. Her garishly painted lips were drawn back from discolored teeth in a grin of evil pleasure.

Then her outstretched hand fisted around the bill which Stockton pressed into it. And the six feet six inch tall, two hundred and fifty pound man snapped his mouth wide to yell: "Stop that killer!"

The Colt was in his left hand and he thrust it high into the air to explode a shot into the night sky as his right arm went forward. The gunshot was heard for a hundred yards along the street in both directions, drawing more than a hundred pairs of eyes toward the man who had fired it. Eyes which saw the outstretched arm and then raked in the direction it indicated.

For perhaps a full two seconds the northwest end of Steuart Street was gripped by a hard, solid silence which seemed to cut it off physically from the rest of the city. Then, out on the bay, a ship's siren wailed to signal the advance of an ocean mist through the Golden Gate. And Stockton and the dozen or more men behind him powered into a run across the street.

"Best not to get involved," Steele said in his

soft Virginia drawl to the closest of the by-standers who gazed at him with a mixture of expressions from shock to curiosity. Then took a two-handed grip on the Colt Hartford and clicked back the hammer.

Men cursed and women gasped. All of them backed hurriedly away from him, as fearful of the guns in the hands of the hunters as of the revolving rifle held by the fugitive. Which left the dudishly attired Virginian isolated in the center of an ever-expanding area of space.

One man, dressed like a cowhand, with the high color of too much liquor inside him, pushed aside the woman who clung to his arm and went for the Frontier Colt in his tied down holster.

Steele vented a mild curse, swung the rifle and squeezed the trigger. The cowhand yelled and fell hard into the gutter, flailing his arms wildly to try to retain his balance as the bullet blasted off the high heel of one of his fancy riding boots.

The shot put everyone else close to Steele to full flight. They whirled and screams and curses filled the warm, salty air as they collided with each other in their haste.

"Move, you bastards, move!" Stockton bellowed, his voice sounding clearly through the noise.

But fear of Steele's gun blinded and deafened everyone to whatever was happening elsewhere on the street. And in the confusion of clamorous

15

sound and panicked movement the Virginian was able to reach the relative safety of another alley. He ran south toward Spear, then made a right turn to emerge onto crowded Market Street. The clatter of running feet and the din of angered voices followed him, the noise amplified by the confines of the building walls to either side.

Traffic was heavy on the slope of Market and drivers yelled abuse at him as he weaved between the carriages and trolleycars. On the far sidewalk he looked back over his shoulder again. And saw the massive Stockton spot him and plunge out into the traffic, trailed by the other men who had left the pleasures of the Bar City bar to join the manhunt.

Aware that only speed could save him from capture, Steele lunged recklessly forward: using a fist, his elbows, and the barrel and stock of the rifle to force a passage through the press of people. Behind him, horses snorted, wheel rims skidded, and vehicles collided as the pursuers streamed across the street. To the left and right of him enraged men and frightened women snarled and shrieked as he charged between them. Some staggered. A few fell. Here and there a man tried to throw a punch or aim a hastily drawn gun. But always there were innocent people shielding the running man.

Steele turned off Market and onto Front Street. No longer running uphill. Heading down toward the waterfront. But his jarred legs did not stop protesting the exertion as he raced along the easier route.

At first there had been anger directed at the gray-bearded man. Then doubt concerned with whether he had made the right decision to run. Now there was fear as he turned first one way and then the other, no longer noticing which street or alley was passing beneath his pumping legs. Always hearing and sometimes seeing the towering figure of Stockton behind him. With the eager group of men at his heels.

But it was not a mindless fear that spread out from the pit of his stomach to reach to his every nerve ending. It was ice cold and firmly controlled, honing his physical reflexes and cooling his mind.

It was during the War Between the States that he had learned to use fear. In such circumstances only a mindless fool did not experience terror of death or a maiming wound that might halt him in his tracks at any moment in the midst of a violent battle or even when he rested in the seeming safety of a camp.

At first, because he was a young man who until the war had experienced only the comfort and privilege of being the son of one of Virginia's wealthiest plantation owners, Adam Steele had attempted to smother terror with bravado. When this failed, he had indulged himself in self-pity. But then he had recognized his responsibilities as a cavalry lieutenant commanding noncoms and troopers.

So it was that he taught himself the only lesson he had to learn from war. Because he already possessed all the other basic skills that were necessary for a junior cavalry officer. For he had spent a great deal of time riding, hunting, and shooting for sport on and around his father's estate. Before the war such skills had been used in the pursuit and killing of game. But for a cause in which he firmly believed, Adam Steele had to surmount only one obstacle before he was able to adapt himself to the slaughter of men.

He rode for the Confederacy, against the Union enemy which was supported by his father.

In time, though, even this fact added to the younger Steele's success as a cavalryman. For as the months of war dragged into years and the prospect of defeat meant the cause was being lost, he was able to fight as fiercely as ever—riding into every battle and toward every skirmish with a vivid image of his father's face imprinted on his mind.

Then came the inevitable end when the opposing generals met at Appomattox Court House with pens instead of sabers and Adam Steele emerged into the peace physically intact but with a mind scarred by guilt. But soon this was eradicated when his father made an overture of reconciliation and the son rode for Washington to meet him, both hopeful to reestablish some semblance of what they had had and what they had been before the start of war.

It was never to be. For men unwilling to accept defeat sought to reopen the conflict. And on the night Lincoln was assassinated, Ben Steele was lynched from a rafter in a barroom. Which caused Adam Steele to fire the first shot in his violent peace.

Since then, when he set out to track down and kill the men who murdered his father, Steele had already been on the run in some way or another. Running away from a fresh guilt at first—because to escape the consequences of avenging his father's death it had been necessary to murder his best friend. Then striving toward a series of objectives: all of them designed to bring him the kind of wealth and position he had enjoyed in his youth. And all of them snatched from his grasp in the midst of bloody violence.

So that just as the cause for which he fought a war was lost, so was his very ambition in the violent peace. And for a long time now he had been on the move simply to survive. Mostly making just enough money to buy the essentials of life. Occasionally, as at the Havelock Hotel, raising a little extra to indulge his never-lost taste for such luxuries as fine clothes.

Now he literally ran for his life, fully aware that if his pursuers got close enough he would be shot down. Maybe killed, or merely wounded—to be taken to jail and there wait to be tried for a hanging crime.

Sweat ran into his eyes to blur his vision and

oozed from his back to paste his clothing to his flesh. There was a dangerous numbness in his legs, swamping the pain to the extent that he could no longer feel them. He could smell the ocean very strongly and received fleeting impressions of high dark buildings, the finger-like jibs of cranes, and the sharply raked prows of moored clippers and smaller craft. His fast-beating heart frenetically pumped blood through his veins and he could hear this drumming in his ears, to the extent that it drowned out all other sounds.

A huge door appeared in front of him. It was painted gray with a dark stripe down one side. He came to a swaying stop and looked back. Along an empty quayside streaked with deep moon shadows. Nothing moved back there. But between gasps for breath he heard shouts and running feet in the distance. He did not trust himself to judge just how far away were the men. He looked again at the towering door and recognized the dark stripe as a gap where it stood open. He had to turn sideways to squeeze through and was immediately enveloped in solid darkness, the impenetrable air heavily redolent with the heady scents of spices.

He staggered forward, holding the Colt Hartford out in front of him, gripping it two-handed as a bar. Whenever the rifle banged against crates or filled sacks he altered course. But always he looked back over his shoulder before he moved again, to ensure that the strip of moonlight at the cracked open door was where he expected it to be.

The deeper he moved into the warehouse, the more muted became the sounds made by his pursuers. Then he reached a point where he could hear only his own breathing and the drumming in his ears. And the crack at the side of the big door was no longer in sight. He sank to the gritty floor and leaned his back and head against a pile of sacks. Painful feeling returned to his legs and his breath whistled out through teeth clenched against the need to groan. His lungs seemed to be filled with glowing embers and his head felt on the point of exploding.

The Havelock Hotel had appeared to be an ideal place for him to rest up after the long trip from Mexico. He had gone to Mexico, he recalled, to try to forget what he had done to Jim Bishop. But that had been another time, many years ago. When he lost for all time his taste for liquor as he tried to drown remorse in whatever kind of alcohol was stocked in the cantina at Nuevo Rio.

This time it had been another village. There had been a mine close by, where an old man died and a young boy did not. He had brought the yong boy home to California becuase it had seemed the right thing to do.

Then there had been the violent time in Sun City which came to an end when he shot the man with the tarnished star. Again it had seemed the right thing to do. But in retrospect he knew he would never be sure whether or not he did the right thing on this occasion.

But at least while he played poker through the nights and slept away the days in the Havelock Hotel he had been able to push such doubt into the back of his mind. As resentment against him built in the minds of everyone who made their living out of what the Bay City Bar had to offer.

He played only poker and never tried any of the games of chance from which the house took percentage.

He drank only coffee, which was supplied free, and never bought hard liquor or beer.

He never took a whore to his room, paid for her drinks, or even purchased a dance ticket.

On the mornings when he came out of a game with a bankroll, he spent it on clothes and meals in classy uptown restaurants and always went to sleep in the cheapest room of the house.

So Madam Mary came to resent his presence. So did her husband. And the bartenders, the croupiers, and the whores. Rod Stockton hated him because the Virginian caused no trouble, just as he hated all Havelock Hotel patrons who behaved themselves.

"Steele!" a man called in a hushed whisper. "Steele! Show yourself, man! We don't aim to do you no harm!"

The Virginian's legs were still paining him but the other discomforts had been soothed out of him by the period of rest against the sacks.

His breathing was normal, the sweat had dried on his face and body, and there was only the faint memory of a dull ache above his left eye.

His gloved hands tightened their grip on the frame and stock of the rifle as he cocked his head: straining to get a bearing on the position of the man who called to him.

"Yeah, Steele! We know you're in here!"

The second man was close to the first and the Virginian used the sound of his voice to cover any slight noise he made in getting to his feet. Both men were in the same general area, to the right of where Steel stood, fresh sweat pumping from his pores.

"We see you come in here! We was trailin' you from the hotel with the others! But we didn't bring that jackass Stockton in here, did we?"

Steele took a cautious step forward, then another one. A draft of damp, ocean-smelling air brushed against his face and he looked to his right. Now that his eyes had adjusted to the darkness he could pick out solid shapes from their backgrounds and saw that he was looking around a crate, down a long aisle between high stacks of other crates, bales, and bulging sacks. At the far end pale moonlight filtered through smoke-like mist to spill a wedge of illumination through the cracked open door of the warehouse.

Two tall, broadly built men showed in moving silhouette against the light as they advanced along the aisle, each with an arm extended out in front of him. They walked slowly, fear dictating their pace and as the stretched arms swung to left and right the metal of revolvers glinted dully in the subdued light.

Then they came to a halt.

"Figure you got us spotted now, Steele! If you ain't, we're ten yards or so in from the door! Got our guns drawn, but now we're gonna put them back in the holsters! You watchin', Steele?"

They did what had been promised, pushing the revolvers under suit jackets into shoulder rigs: and then raised both arms above their heads, fingers splayed to show they were empty-handed.

"Want to make a deal with you, Steele! You're in big trouble and we can get you out of it! You do a job for us and we'll make sure you get safe passage out of the city! You watchin', Steele?"

The man doing most of the talking was on the left from the Virginian's viewpoint. Slightly the taller of the two but not so broad across the shoulders and chest. He wore a Stetson while the other man had a derby set on his head at a jaunty angle.

"Brad here's gonna strike a match," the taller man called, his voice not so loud now, as both of them lowered their arms. "Sign of good faith. Like us puttin' up our guns. Okay, Brad."

The Virginian knew he had to take a calculated risk and trust the men. For if the whole bunch who had followed him out of the Havelock Hotel knew he was in the warehouse, Rod Stockton would still be calling the shots. He was that kind of man. He was also the kind of man who would launch a full-scale attack rather than attempt a subtle trick.

Steele squeezed his eyes closed as the match was struck on the cement floor of the warehouse. Opened them when the initial flare had become a flicker: the match held at shoulder level between the two men to dance its light on the sides of their faces. The faces of men in their thirties, Brad at least five years younger than the man who did most of the talking.

Brad was clean-shaven, the other man sporting a bushy black moustache that dipped down low to each side of his broad mouth. Both of them vaguely familiar to Steele, who had seen them most nights in the Bay City bar: drinking in moderation and occasionally playing a little poker. Never in the same game that occupied him.

He stepped out into the aisle before the match was burned a quarter of the way down its length, clicking back the hammer of the rifle and aiming it from the hip at the older man.

"Can hear and see, fellers," he drawled as he moved slowly toward the two men, who expressed fear as he showed himself and then sighed their relief through teeth bared in strained smiles. "You have anybody covering

25

me, I reckon I'll have company on the trip to hell. We could even go three-handed."

"Forget that idea, Steele. Name's Dwight Newman. This here's Bradley Engles. You must have seen us around the hotel."

The Virginian halted twenty feet away from them and nodded. "Saw Stockton there, too. He wouldn't . . ."

"Stockton worked there," Newman interrupted as Engles dropped the match just before it started to burn his finger and thumb. But there was still enough misty moonlight entering the warehouse for Steele to have a clear view of his potential target. "It's his job to get you for what you done to that Chink whore. Me and Brad was just customers. More interested in you than the whores, the booze, and the gamblin'."

Steele pursed his lips. "The rumors aren't true. Just because I don't go with whores . . ."

The memory of the dull ache above his left eye was suddenly revived. Became an excruciating agony that filled his entire head. His brain was still imprinted with the words to complete the sentence: ". . . you shouldn't believe those fairy tales."

His mouth opened to speak the words, but all that emerged was a strangled groan as he crumpled to the floor.

Chapter Three

"I AM very sorry that I hit you so hard, Adam Steele. But it seemed the only thing we could do. For you are not a man with a trusting nature, are you?"

The Virginian had opened his eyes and seen just a jumbled, blurred pattern of light and shade. Then the pain that seemed powerful enough to split his skull had intensified and he snapped the lids closed again. The words the woman spoke to him sounded as if they came from a long way off, called down a tunnel to reach his ears as a faint whisper.

"There is a bruise but the skin is not broken. Your hat and hair softened the blow. Our doctor says there will be pain for a while but it will go away soon. There should be no lasting effects."

The voice was louder now, each word spoken by the woman penetrating his brain like a hot needle, triggering a fresh pulse of agony.

"You are still awake, Adam Steele?"

This question hit him like a series of palpable blows. And he felt hot breath on the side of his face. His nostrils filled with the smell of chili. He opened his eyes again and gritted his teeth against the pain as the component parts of the confused pattern moved and abruptly became crystal clear. The thin, lined face of a gray-haired old woman moving up and away from his; a whitened ceiling with a kerosene lamp hanging from a hook; the chests, shoulders, and heads of three men.

"Sure he is, Martha," one of the men said, his voice as boomingly loud as that of the woman. "He's comin' outta it real fine this time."

"You're the wrong side of my skull to have any opinion, Newman," the Virginian growled, recognizing the man with the moustache.

The first few words he spoke seemed like the loudest sounds he had ever heard in his life. But then his senses reverted to normal. The slightest noise no longer battered his ears, the texture of the blanket he lay on lost its roughness, he saw his surroundings less vividly, the smells of old cooking and fresh body odor became less rancid and the foul taste in his mouth lost its nauseating edge.

He was aware of restraints at his wrists and ankles and swung and raised his head—saw that he was spread-eagled with hands and feet tied to bedposts. His suit jacket and vest had been removed and he saw them draped over a chair by a bureau, with his hat resting on top. The knife from the boot sheath lay on the brim of the hat. His Colt Hartford leaned against the chair.

"If you did not hear everything Mrs. Craig said, *señor*, I will repeat it. She apologizes on behalf of us all for the necessity to hit you on the head. It was most unfortunate but the doctor . . ."

"Reckons I should live," the Virginian cut in on the young Mexican, still having to speak through gritted teeth as the pain of the blow diminished from a constant peak and started to attack in waves. "If you can call this living. Seems like I was right to have a distrustful nature."

He shifted his half-open eyes away from the Mexican, who was in his mid-twenties—tall and slim and almost handsome except for a livid line of scar tissue on the right side of his jaw which gave his mouth a cruel twist. To glance coldly over the faces of the taller Newman and Engles, who returned his survey with bleak looks of their own.

"I felt you would not take kindly to the proposition we have to put to you, Adam Steele," Martha Craig said.

She was in her late sixties, perhaps even past seventy. Almost six feet tall and very thin.

Dressed in a close-fitting black dress that emphasized the prominent bone structure of her emaciated body and the almost cadaverous pallor of her face.

"You're light on your feet, ma'am," he told her sourly.

She sank out of sight and he had to crane his neck to the side to see her now that she had sat down on a chair to the right of the bedstead. "I think we were lucky," she replied with a slight lift of her narrow shoulders, the expression of misery on her wasted features not altering. "It had been a bad time for you. You could not be expected to have all your wits about you. We were also lucky that you made your escape in this direction. So that it did not take long for Bradley to fetch Angelo and me while Dwight watched that you did not leave the warehouse."

"The man with the gray beard work for you, too?"

She showed a puzzled frown now, which gave some life to her pale blue eyes beneath her deeply lined forehead. "What man?"

"The one who killed the Havelock Hotel whore."

She shook her head and the thin, white hair moved hardly at all about her ears. But the gesture was not a reply to his question. "Do not try to deny us our good fortune, Adam Steele. Dwight and Bradley were only two of many witnesses who heard the Chinese girl name you with her dying breath."

"And an innocent man does not run away, *señor*," Angelo added morosely. "Please listen to the deal which Mrs. Craig will put to you."

"Or I'll hit you harder than she did, punk!" Brad Engles snapped. "And I won't need no length of timber to do it."

He punched a clenched fist into an open palm as he formed his bronzed features into a brutal sneer.

"Shut your trap," Newman warned him coldly and drew a glare of hot anger which withered under the power of his own steady gaze. "Tell the man, Martha."

The old woman nodded. "Dwight and Bradley have been watching you for several days, Adam Steele. And have formed certain opinions of you. Had the shooting of the Chinese girl not happened, it was still planned that you and I should talk tonight."

"Whether I wanted to or not?" Steele asked.

Another rise and fall of the old woman's thin shoulders. "When people are sufficiently dedicated, there is little they cannot do. Earlier you saw Dwight and Bradley in a conciliatory attitude. Just now you glimpsed another side of Bradley. And Dwight can be even more persuasive." She raised her hands and waved them across her sparse breasts. "But we are wasting time with might-have-beens. The Chinese girl was killed and you are now being hunted for shooting her. Which gives us an unexpected card in our hand. All other factors are as they

31

were. Primarily that you have no money and that your main source of income is derived from your skill with the rifle that never leaves your side."

"The first we know is true, Steele," Newman put in. "The second is what me and Brad decided after watchin' you so long."

"I do all kinds of things to earn a dollar, feller," the Virginian replied, subduing an impulse to guess at the reason for his captivity. Since it was a futile mental exercise.

"It is five thousand dollars which we have in mind, Adam Steele," Martha Craig said.

"To kill how many people?"

"Just one."

"You just keep Newman and Engles around to form opinions, ma'am?"

"We ain't 'kept around' for nothin', punk!" the younger man snarled.

"Go get some coffee, Brad!" the moustached Newman growled and his partner hesitated only a moment before he whirled and strode across the room, using the door as an outlet for some of his anger. The kerosene lamp swayed in the wake of the hard slam. Then Newman sat on the side of the bed and sighed as he gazed bleakly down into the Virginian's face. "Him and me have killed a lot of men, Steele. In our trade it happens that way. We're bounty hunters: and if the flyers say 'dead or alive' we ain't never been choosy which it is. But most of the time we use handguns. We ain't no marksmen with rifles. Seen how you don't carry no hand-gun. Seen you always with a Colt Hartford which is a rifle for a man who knows he's good. On account of it not firin' so fast or so many shells as the Winchester. And since the man we want killed won't ever get close enough to be in re-volver range, it's a job for a rifleman. A damn good rifleman. If it wasn't that way, we sure as hell would be happy to keep our share of the five grand and take care of Vettori ourselves."

He stood up from the bed, went to the chair in the corner, swept Steele's coat, vest, hat, and knife to the floor and sat down. Then he crossed his arms and compressed his lips to em-phasize that he had said his piece.

"Hernando Vettori, *señor*," the scarred Mexi-can added bitterly, running two fingers along the disfigurement on his jaw. "Probably you have never heard of him?"

"Which is a good reason for me not to kill him I reckon, feller," the Virginian replied.

"You will kill him, Adam Steele," the old woman said resolutely. "Now that the alterna-tive is to be hanged for the murder of a harlot."

Angelo seemed not to hear Mrs. Craig's com-ment as he continued to massage the livid tissue on his face and stare at the crucifix hanging above the cracked mirror of the bureau behind the old woman. "He is now a minister in the government of Mexico City. But once, not so long ago, Vettori was a *Federale* officer, com-manding the post at Guerrero, a village in Senora high in the Sierra Madres. It was there that he signed his own death warrant, in the blood of others, which you will carry out."

"Unless we have made a serious misjudgment, Adam Steele."

A booted foot crashed against the door and Newman reached across to open it. Engles, looking disgusted at having to undertake the chore, carried a laden tray into the room and set it on the bureau. There were just four mugs on the tray, besides a large, fire-blackened coffee pot with aromatic smoke wisping out of the spout.

"I think that we have not," Angelo announced, bringing his mind back from out of the past and speaking as confidently as the old woman had a few moments previously. "For I am sure there is some small amount of compassion beneath the hard shell which Señor Steele shows to the world."

Engles went to squat down on his haunches on the other side of the door from where Newman sat on the chair. He took out a cheroot, lit it, and snorted smoke out through his nostrils.

"Keep it shut, Brad," his partner warned. "We done all we had to for now."

"So why do you not leave us?" Angelo suggested.

"Who asked you, Mex?" Engles snarled, powering upright and staring his vicious anger at the young Mexican.

"Bradley!" Martha Craig bellowed, with surprising force for such a slightly built and old woman.

"It's okay, Martha," Newman said evenly, controlling his own rage so that the only overt sign of it was a glitter in his green eyes as he rose slowly off the chair. Then, as he made to open the door, his movements suddenly became fast. He was already perfectly balanced and in the right position, but Engles was still directing scorn toward the frightened Angelo. And was taken totally by surprise as the clenched right fist of his partner crashed into the side of his jaw.

"I warned you, Brad!" Newman said in the same unemotional tone as the younger man staggered across the room, hit the wall, and half fell to the floor. "These people are our friends."

As he recovered, Engles instinctively moved a hand to reach under his jacket lapel. Then froze the action as the older man growled:

"You ain't that stupid!"

The words were enough, for Newman kept both his hands low down at his sides: far removed from the revolver in the shoulder holster.

Engles's flushed face held its expression of rage for a moment longer, then showed a mixture of resentment and humiliation as he shifted his gaze from Angelo to Steele, to Martha Craig, and finally looked at Newman—but could not hold the level gaze of his partner for more than a second.

"Hell, Dwight," he muttered as he stepped on the smoking cheroot that had been knocked from his lips. "You know I don't like takin' no orders from anyone 'cept you."

Newman opened the door and jerked a thumb through it. "So take one. I said we done all we had to for now." Then he grinned as Engles chanced a glance at him. "Let's go down and have ourselves a snort, old buddy."

Engles showed a smile like that of a relieved child let off the hook by an indulgent parent. And avoided looking at anyone else in the room as he went out.

The door closed behind the two bounty hunters and Martha Craig sighed. "Cut one of his hands free and then pour the coffee, Angelo," she instructed. "And you must try not to provoke that oaf, my dear."

The Mexican, who was dressed in the same city style as Newman and Engles, but looked uncomfortably out of place in the attire, reached under his jacket at the back to draw a short-bladed knife. Anxiety continued to show on his sweat-beaded face as he stooped over the bed, his hands shaking.

"Be grateful if you'd wait awhile, feller," Steele drawled. "Way you are now you could cut my wrist instead of the rope."

"Do not mock my grandson," the old woman

36

instructed sadly. "First you should listen to what we have to tell you before you reach conclusions about any of us."

The final strands of the rope were severed and Steele was able to move his left hand to his head and probe through the hair to touch the large contusion on his scalp.

"I'm tied down to listening, ma'am," he muttered. "But I'll be doing it under sufferance."

Mrs. Craig set her thin, bloodless lips into a tight line as Angelo began to pour coffee from the pot into three of the mugs. Then: "If that is meant to be some clever play on words, young man, I will tell you that you do not know the meaning of suffering."

"I do not think that is so, Mrs. Craig," her grandson said as he gave her a mug of coffee. "I think Señor Steele has endured much hardship throughout his life."

The Virginian took the offered mug of coffee in his freed hand with a nod of thanks. Then returned his attention to the emaciated old woman as she momentarily lost her composure and vented a low sound of impatience.

"We're not here to talk about my problems, Angelo," he drawled.

"If you consent to do as we ask, you will have none, Adam Steele. Some time tomorrow afternoon a ship will dock at the Filbert Street Pier and Hernando Vettori will disembark to be greeted by the governor of California on behalf of the president. There will be many guards, but Mexican and American, for we are not alone in having reason to hate the evil monster. So only an expert marksman capable of firing a long-range rifle shot will be able to kill him.

"We have made careful arrangements to ensure that the marksman will remain safely concealed until he fires the shot. And that there will be adequate time for him to withdraw from his position and escape from the city after the deed is done."

"With five thousand dollars in his pocket," Angelo added as his grandmother raised the mug to her lips, having to hold it in both thin hands.

"Precisely so. And I fail to see how you can refuse to do this for us, Adam Steele. If you are what Dwight has told me you are. A man who lives by the gun. Of whom he has known many. And in addition to the money we are willing to pay, there is an additional incentive. In that we will guarantee you escape the consequences of what happened at the Havelock Hotel earlier tonight."

"And, of course, Señor Steele," the Mexican augmented anxiously, "no one will ever know it was you who rid the world of the ogre Hornando Vettori."

"What do you say?"

The old woman and the young Mexican both watched with intense eyes as the Virginian sipped at the hot coffee, his bronzed and lined face giving no clue to his thoughts.

He lowered the mug and pursed his lips. "Say I'm a much sought-after feller, ma'am. One way or the other, everyone wants me for murder."

Chapter Four

"NOT MURDER, *señor*," the Mexican girl corrected mournfully as she pushed open the door with one hand, skillfully balancing a tray on the splayed palm of the other. "You will be carrying out a sentence of execution on a torturer and mass murderer."

She was in her mid-twenties. Five feet three inches tall and weighing no more than a hundred pounds. She wore a black dress as close-fitting as that of the old woman but with a neckline low enough to reveal the start of the rises and valley of her firmly jutting breasts. It was also shorter, reaching midway down her slender calves above feet that were bare of shoes and hose. Her features possessed a fragile beauty, with large black eyes, a delicately shaped nose between gently curved cheeks and full, wide lips. Her flawless skin was light olive brown and her hair which was parted in the middle and fell to the shoulders to frame the face was jet black, with a luxuriant sheen in the lamplight.

As she moved to the bureau and set down the tray her finely flared hips swayed with a natural, unaffected grace.

"We thought you would be hungry, *señor*," she announced, her tone matter-of-fact after the venom which had dripped from her opening words. She removed one plate from the top of another and released steam and the appetizing aroma of fried chicken into the room.

She smiled with white, perfect teeth.

"We know you have not eaten since you spent most everything you had on breakfast early this morning," Mrs. Craig added. "This is Renita, who is a fine cook."

"*Señorita*," Steele greeted as the girl carried the plate of food and a fork around the foot of the bed and set them down on the blanket beside his left hip.

As she stooped, the neckline of the dress sagged to expose the full extent of the valley between her breasts. The way she held the pose for part of a second too long showed that the display had been deliberate.

"Anything you people don't know about me?" he asked as he looked briefly into the big eyes of Renita, saw they were as implacable as his own, and handed her his empty mug.

"Much," the old woman replied as the girl began to collect all the mugs and return them to the tray. "Most important is the point which Angelo touched on earlier. Namely, whether a man such as you possesses compassion."

The fried chicken was accompanied by grits and black-eyed peas. All of it tasted good. Steele ate the food and avoided looking at the swaying figure of Renita as the girl carried both trays and all the used utensils out of the room. When she had closed the door behind her, he asked:

"You reckon that's what it takes for one man to kill another he doesn't even know, ma'am?"

Impatience threatened her composure again. "Do not pretend to be obtuse, young man!" she snapped, then shook her head. "I'm sorry. We cannot hope to ingratiate ourselves with you. But rancor will not achieve our object, either."

"I will tell him, Mrs. Craig?"

"It was what we agreed, Angelo. You were there and I was not."

The Mexican went to get the chair Newman had used, brought it to the side of the bed and sat down. "It is a terrible story I have to tell, Señor Steele. The things which I have to speak of will not put you off your food?"

"When I'm hungry and there's something to eat, I eat it, feller."

"Si. You are of a kind with Señor Newman and Señor Engles."

The Virginian sighed. "You've got a captive

audience, feller. But insults like that will get you nowhere fast."

Angelo looked perturbed.

"Get on with it," his grandmother urged.

"*Si*. It is now almost three years since Hernando Vettori committed the crimes for which he must die. In the village of Guerrero where I lived with my mother who was Mexican and my father who was the son of Mrs. Craig. My father was the priest. Renita also lived in Guerrero with her mother and father who was the storekeeper. The *señores* Newman and Engles did not live in the village but often they stayed in the cantina when they were not out in the mountains hunting for bandits and for American criminals."

He glanced tentatively across the bed and prisoner at Martha Craig, seeking her approval. He was starting to sweat.

"You are doing just fine, my dear," she encouraged.

Angelo licked his lips and grimaced at the salty taste. "It was a good village in which to live, *señor*. The people were poor, but they were kind and they helped each other in times of need. And we were never troubled by bandits because of the *Federale* post that guarded the pass in which was Guerrero. Until one day when many bandits attacked the post. It was early in the morning and the rain fell very heavily. The soldiers were taken by surprise and all of them were killed. Twenty-five officers and men, *señor*. Not only killed, but their corpses mutilated and hung by ropes from the tops of the fort walls. Some were not dead but only wounded when the bandits used their knives."

The young Mexican no longer looked at either Steele or his grandmother. Instead, he gazed with frowning eyes at the crucifix above the bureau, as if tacitly imploring the deity it represented to explain how such atrocities could be allowed.

"We villagers could do nothing, *señor*. We had no weapons and also we were held captive in the church of my father while the attack took place. And after the bandits had left Guerrero, we still did not dare do anything. For the leader of the band said that if we cut even one soldier down from the wall he would bring his men back again. And kill everyone who lived in the village."

Steele finished eating, rattled the fork down on the plate and rested his dully aching head on the pillow, fixing his impassive gaze on the ceiling.

"Perhaps we were cowards, *señor*. But we did as we were ordered. We lived for six days with the stench of the many dead reaching into every corner of every house. Then, after the buzzards and flies had picked the flesh from the bones of the dead, another four days passed before Hernando Vettori came to Guerrero with *Federales*. Brought there by the *señores* Newman and Engles who had ridden through the village while the dead still had flesh on their bones to show the wounds they suffered."

The lamp had started to dim as Angelo began his story. Now, as the flame exhausted the last of the kerosene from the wick, the light failed completely and the room was plunged into pitch darkness, for there was no window in any wall.

"Continue, Angelo," Martha Craig encouraged dully. "I prefer this. It is better than having to look at a man who remains totally unmoved by what you are telling him."

"That sounds like rancor again, ma'am," Steele drawled.

"For which I will not apologize, young man," the old woman responded, her voice sounding even more cultured in the solid darkness. "I cannot pretend to be like you. I have feelings."

"So have I, ma'am. And you hurt them."

"But you will recover from your minor injury. Unlike more than half the villagers of Guerrero. Finish your story, Angelo. Although I fear it will serve no purpose and that we will have to rely on the threat of hanging."

The chair legs scraped on the floorboards as Martha Craig rose to her feet. And she groaned softly, as if it pained her ancient joints to support all her weight after she had been seated for so long. Steele sensed her standing over him as the Mexican began to talk again. Faster than before, as if he was anxious to be through with reviving old and tormenting memories.

"Vettori accused us of cowardice and disrespect for the dead and not one of us who lived in the village could deny this, *señor*. Then he took his men out into the hills for many days, to search for the bandits who did the killing. But he failed to find them and this made him very angry. For, we learned later, his promotion from captain to major depended on bringing the murderers to justice.

"For a whole week he remained in the post. And when he emerged it was a black day for Guerrero. Perhaps we shall never know whether it was simply spite or a genuine belief that we villagers aided the bandits. But Vettori sent his men to bring us all to the fort. Some said he was drunk but I think he was sick—in the head because he had failed. He stood us all in a line against a wall, with his men aiming their rifles at us. And demanded to know where the bandits were hidden.

"My father protested and was shot before he had spoken more than a few words."

Martha Craig vented a shuddering sob, then uttered a strange croaking sound that served to bring her emotions under control. "Go on, Angelo," she insisted hoarsely as the Mexican gulped.

"Vettori walked up to my father, the priest of Guerrero, drew his pistol and shot him in the center of the face from no more than two feet away. There was much noise and movement, which ended when the soldiers fired their rifles into the air. Then all the women were ordered to step out of the line and Vettori threatened to have them shot down if the men did not reveal where the bandits were hiding. The monster himself aimed his pistol at Renita who was the most beautiful woman in our village.

"It was because of her that Señor Newman attempted to halt the killing. For he had a deep affection for her. He and Señor Engles were not in the line, you understand. They were watching from the gates of the post. But two men faced with so many could do nothing. Vettori counted to ten and all we could do was implore him to believe that we did not know where the bandits were hiding and had not aided them when they attacked the Guerrero post.

"He gave the order to fire and every woman except for Renita was killed. No one believed he would do it, señor. Or there was hope his men would refuse to obey him. But the slaughter occurred, in front of the eyes of the men and children of the village. We were gripped by the madness of fury then, señor. Each of us individually. No one person made the first move. No one spoke through the grief in his throat. But every man moved forward, leaving the children weeping over the corpses of their mothers.

"At first the *Federales* fired bullets above our heads. But when this did not halt us, they fired at us. I and a handful of others were fortunate. We fell to the ground wounded rather than dead. Those of us who were still able to move struggled to reach the *Federales*. But it was futile. They used their rifles or pistols to club us senseless. The scar on my face was caused by a blow from Vettori's own pistol.

"Before the ogre came to Guerrero seventy-nine men, women, and children lived in the village, *señor*. After the slaughter, only ten men remained alive, including myself. All the children. And Renita.

"But she remained under threat of death. For Vettori ordered the two American bounty hunters to go into the mountains and search for the bandits' hideout. If they had not returned within seven days with information on the whereabouts of the bandits, she would have been executed.

"She lives still because they did return to Guerrero, *señor*. And were able to lead the ogre and his men to the place. No prisoners were taken. The bandits were shot down as brutally as they had killed the *Federales* who used to be at the Guerrero post.

"We heard of this from the *señores* Newman and Engles who narrowly escaped with their own lives after the bandits were all dead. For Vettori wanted no one left alive who knew of the events at Guerrero.

"But some of us are still alive, *señor*. The bounty hunters, the men who survived that terrible day, and the children. We scattered far and wide after the bounty hunters returned to the village to warn us. And a few of us have come together here to ensure that Hernando Vettori pays with his life for what he did that day."

Martha Craig had been shuffling up and down the room as Angelo told his story, as if she felt that movement would help her to handle grief for her long-dead son and daughter-in-law. Now she sighed as she sat down again beside the bed.

"There is little more to tell, Adam Steele," she said. "Vettori was hailed as a hero for finding and killing the bandits. The massacre doubly welcomed since he and his men placed the blame for the slaughter at Guerrero upon the bandits.

"It is, of course, impossible to accept that all the men under his command were as inhuman as he during the killing of the villagers. But time heals most things, including tormented consciences. And each man was rewarded with more than mere medals. As Vettori gained rapid promotion through the Mexican military, he saw to it that all those who served with him at Guerrero also gained success in their careers." She paused, then raised her voice. "You are listening, aren't you, young man?"

"To every word, ma'am," Steele assured her.

"Good. Naturally, the survivors from the village attempted to make the truth known. But no one in Mexico City would listen to mostly illiterate *peones* and two American bounty hunters. Do you know Mexico?"

"I've been down there a few times, ma'am."

"Then you will know that civilians have a low regard for the *Federales*. And that so-called *gringo* bounty hunters are despised by all. So there never was the remotest possibility that the truth would be accepted from such people.

"The children have always been helpless, of course. Because of their age. Perhaps the men still harbor hope of revenge but we do not know where they are. They do not matter at this moment. Here in San Francisco there are five of us with reason to hate Hernando Vettori who have waited for a long time to strike a blow on behalf of all who died or suffered at Guerrero. And we ask you to help us. For financial reward and for your life."

The legs of the chair scraped the floor again as she stood up.

"Come, Angelo. We will leave him now to think of what we have told him. Consider carefully, Adam Steele. We have no reason to lie to you, as I am sure you will accept. But even if you have no sympathy for us, you cannot afford to refuse our offer. Unless you are tired of living and ready to die on the gallows."

She had shuffled across to the door. When she opened it, a faint glow of lamplight, subdued by distance, crept weakly into the room. She showed in lone silhouette against it for a moment, then was joined by Angelo. Since hearing that the young Mexican had been wounded in the massacre at his native village,

Steele noticed he limped, favoring his right leg.

"Do you wish me to refuel the lamp, *señor*? And light it for you?"

"There's nothing here I want to see, feller," the Virginian replied, hearing a short smattering of mumbled talk from elsewhere in the building.

"Least of all our point of view, I feel," Martha Craig responded morosely, ushering her grandson out of the room ahead of her. Then she closed the door gently and a key rattled in the lock.

"Can see that all right, lady," he rasped against the diminishing sound of their receding footfalls going down a stairway. He reached across his body with his released left hand to work on the knotted rope restraining the right one. "But all I want to feel is free."

Chapter Five

HE SWEATED in the darkness of the room as he resisted the impulse to work frenetically at the knotted rope. He had to take a chance on how much time would be allowed him before the group realized the mistakes they had made—in not tying his left wrist to the bedpost again and in leaving his knife and the Colt Hartford on the floor by the door.

So it was the sweat of tension rather than exertion that oozed from his pores as he fumbled with the tightly knotted rope, straining his ears to pick up the first sound of a tread outside the door.

Time played tricks in the silent darkness with each minute seeming to stretch far beyond its allotted span before the rope loosened at the tug of his fingers and he was able to draw his right wrist out of the bond. Then, sitting up and stretching forward, it was easier to unfasten the knots at his ankles because he could use both hands.

His head stopped aching while he was occupied with freeing himself, but then the effects of the blow began to hammer at the underside of his skull again. And the old pains in his legs made themselves felt as he swung his feet gently to the floor and eased himself upright.

When his captors had moved around the room he had not been aware of any creaks from the boarding under their weight. Now, each step that he took toward where his clothes and weapons lay produced a sound of tortured timber that seemed loud enough to be heard throughout the building.

Nobody came to investigate. When he pressed his ear to the door panel only silence beat against the drum.

He slid the knife through the split in his pants seam and into the boot sheath first. Then, before he donned the vest and suit jacket, he unknotted his necktie and unfastened the top two buttons of his shirt. Underneath was a gray silk kerchief which hung loosely around his neck. He pulled out, over his shirt, the two weighted corners—diagonally opposite each other—which, in the right circumstances, made the innocent-looking piece of material as deadly a weapon as the knife and rifle. For the scarf was, in fact, a weapon: which he had taken from the corpse of one of the Oriental thugs he had been forced to kill when seeking revenge for the murder of his father.

Then, fully dressed, and with the cocked rifle held two-handed across his thighs, he sat in one of the chairs which he placed four feet away from the door and slightly to the left of it.

And filled his mind with irrelevant thoughts—to combat the urge to hot anger which threatened to trigger reckless action.

Since the lynching of his father, he understood well the powerful impulses sparked by the desire for revenge. So, given that he believed the story Angelo Craig had told him—and as the young man's grandmother had pointed out, there had been no point in lying—he could understand why his captors wanted to kill Hernando Vettori.

Perhaps had they approached him openly, he might have seriously considered doing what they asked. For five thousand dollars and a way out of the city—or even the money, if they had put their proposition before the whore was murdered at the Havelock Hotel.

He shook his head, feeling the cold ball of anger in the pit of his stomach begin to glow with the threat of hot rage. No, that could never have been. He had firmly established one principle in his mind after a violent trip up the Mississippi and Red Rivers many months ago. He was a skilled killer, but not the kind who took life purely for financial reward in isolation. He killed only to defend himself and in order to complete whatever job he had undertaken.

This one principle above all others—few others if he should consider such issues deeply—was all that raised him, in his own estimation, above the level of the men who lynched his father. Or the gray-bearded man who shot a defenseless Chinese whore. Dwight Newman and Bradley Engles who hunted for bounty—as the Virginian once had himself—but did not care whether they were paid for a prisoner or a corpse. And Hernando Vettori.

The thoughts that ran through Steele's mind were futile time fillers because, if he would never have accepted such a job before, he was certainly in no mood to agree to do it after the pain and humiliation he had been forced to suffer.

Then, as he heard a step on the floor beyond the locked door, he felt his lips part to form the line of a vicious grin. As he relished a sudden thought which flashed unannounced into his fast-working mind. His code did not allow him to make a long-range killing shot at the Mexican who would arrive in the city tomorrow. But in the name of personal revenge and the need to escape, he could feel fully justified in blasting, stabbing, or strangling to death everyone who stood in his way.

Then he compressed his lips as the key turned in the lock the moment the feet ceased to slap at the floor. Feet rather than boots or shoes. But despite the fact that he knew it was the barefoot Renita who was about to swing open the door, he remained resolutely determined to squeeze the Colt Hartford trigger if he even suspected it was necessary. And he did not alter his mind even when the door cracked open to more than an inch and the woman whispered:

"Adam? Adam Steele? Did you get yourself free yet?"

He stood up slowly from the chair and on this occasion the floor did not protest at bearing his weight. Then aimed the rifle in one hand while he reached out with the other. Grasped the handle. Wrenched open the door.

She squealed her alarm and was jerked halfway over the threshold before she released the handle on her side of the door. She saw the muzzle of the Colt Hartford less than six inches from her face and became like a statue in an awkward stance: legs splayed, torso folded forward and arms hanging down so that her hands almost brushed the floor. Her big dark eyes peered fearfully out through the strands of her richly textured hair.

"You can see for yourself," he rasped.

"Please, I come to help you, Adam," she whispered, fear of his grim expression and the closeness of the rifle muzzle raising a lump in her throat. "It is stupid, what they try to make you do."

"One area of agreement doesn't mean a lasting friendship, Renita," he told her. "But if you show me the way out of here I'll return the favor. I won't kill you."

She straightened up, very slowly, afraid that any sudden movement might be misinterpreted. "That is why I came up to the room. To free you if you had not taken advantage of the rope Angelo cut. And to let you out of the house now that the others have gone."

"Where?"

She shook her head, hair brushing across her face. "Best that we talk later, Adam. First we should leave this place."

She was no longer afraid of him but her expression as she turned to start along the hallway showed a deeper fear of those she was betraying. That was how the Virginian chose to explain her attitude as he followed her slender form. But he continued to keep the Colt Hartford cocked, his finger on the trigger and the muzzle trained at the center of her back.

The hallway was about twenty feet long with one closed door either side. Then they went down the stairs, which were uncarpeted. The woman moved in almost total silence but Steele could not prevent his boots rapping on the bare boards. The source of the light which rose up the stairs and along the hallway was a room beyond an open doorway off a lobby below. There were no furnishings in the lobby. Cleaner patches of white on the grubby walls showed where pictures had once hung.

"Hold it," Steele instructed, halting the Mexican girl in her tracks as she made for the front door which had a panel of stained glass pieces in the upper panel.

"Please, we must be quick, Adam," Renita implored.

The Virginian stepped onto the threshold of the lighted room and raked his dark eyes over the place. It was as spartanly furnished as the room in which he had been a prisoner. Just a table and four chairs in the center, two unfurled bedrolls along the foot of a wall, and a sideboard. All the furniture was old and battered. The lamp stood on the table, surrounded by dirty mugs and glasses. A low fire in the cooking range set into a recess generated a little heat. The room smelled of coffee, tobacco smoke, and strong liquor.

"Adam!"

"Go ahead," he allowed and she sighed her relief as she hurried to the door, opened it, and peered outside.

Cool air wafted salt-carrying tendrils of ocean mist around her body and into the building.

"Come," she urged, and beckoned with her hand.

"You've got no shoes on," Steele pointed out.

"It is how I like to be."

She stepped outside and he followed her, keeping the rifle trained on her back as he looked quickly to left and right. Then made a more careful survey. The mist was not thick: little more than a damp haze that allowed the almost full moon to drop a blue-tinged light on the street and its flanking buildings. The gentle breeze that stirred the mist and gave it a saline taste was coming from the right, cooling the sweat of tension on the faces of the woman and the man as they stood at the top of a short flight of stone steps.

"Where are we?" he asked after he had seen no lighted windows and no sign of human presence along the length of the street. Except for that which spilled into the lobby behind them. "Talk as you go."

She led him down the eight steps and then turned right, toward the waterfront. "Still in the city. The name of this street is Vallejo. We are between Battery and Front Streets."

It was an area of three-story brownstone houses, all of them outwardly identical to the one they had just left, with railed steps up to the front doors and basement wells on either side in blocks of four with narrow alleys between the blocks. The open doorway which spilled mist-blurred yellow light and the couple moving along the sidewalk away from it gave life to surroundings that would otherwise have looked totally abandoned.

"What time is it, Renita?"

"Very late. Or very early."

"Where have they gone?"

"To the area of the pier where Vettori's ship will dock."

"And us?"

"Away from the city, of course. I have thought much of how to do this, and have decided that we should steal a small boat and cross the bay to Oakland. There we will be able to take a train. I do not think they will suspect us of leaving San Francisco in such a way."

At the intersection with Front Street she halted and raised an arm across his chest. Both of them peered to left and right: at the darkened façades of saloons, dancehalls, small hotels, boarding houses, and stores. The sidewalks beneath the jumble of signs were in deep shadow. The broad street was moonlit and empty. Time played tricks again, stretching the sweating seconds it took them to cross the street. And Steele's footfalls sounded dangerously loud. The Colt Hartford had not threatened the woman since she started down the steps of the brownstone. Now the Virginian continued to swing it to left and right in the same arc as his peering eyes.

Some of the tension drained out of them as they reached the opposite sidewalk and continued to head eastward toward the intersection with Davis Street, the smell of the ocean now permeated with the stink of rotten fish.

"You think it is a good method to escape the city, Adam?" Renita asked.

"A dangerous way."

"All ways will be dangerous. When a man is wanted for murder."

"Reckon so. But San Francisco Bay isn't a stream."

"If you wish something else, Adam, I will agree. But you will take me with you, won't you? They will be very angry that I helped you escape. I think they will be angry enough to kill me."

"Damn right, bitch!" Bradley Engles snarled, stepping from a doorway ten feet ahead of them and thrusting forward a Smith and Wesson .38. Aimed at the woman.

The fear that had been building up as she made her plea to Steele abruptly became too much for her to bear. She pulled her lips wide to vent a scream, but collapsed in a faint before she could voice it.

Engles's gun followed her down.

As the muzzle of another revolver touched cold metal to the nape of the Virginian's neck.

"I'll kill you and be a hero, Steele," Dwight Newman rasped. "The law will like me for savin' them some trouble. And I figure I'll be able to drink free for life in the Bay City bar. She was real popular, that whore you killed."

Steele froze, the rifle aimed at Engles. They were in front of an office building ideally suited for such a trap to be set and sprung—Engles emerging from the porch as Newman came out of the deeply shadowed alley at the side.

"Which would mean all our planning had

been for nothing, Adam Steele," Martha Craig said morosely, as she stepped from the doorway to stand beside the tense and sour-looking Engles. "But there will be other opportunities to assassinate Vettori. You will have no opportunities for anything."

The Virginian heard footfalls behind him and realized that Newman had removed his boots in order to get so close to his objective. Angelo Craig had remained concealed in the alley until the recapture was almost complete.

"Please surrender, *señor*," he requested in his mournful voice. "The alternative will not achieve anything for anybody."

"Steele ain't stupid, kid," Newman rasped. "He knows that. Get his rifle and that knife outta the trick sheath. You gonna let him do that?"

The cold ring of metal that was the revolver muzzle applied greater pressure to the Virginian's neck.

Renita groaned her subconscious decision to begin coming out of her faint.

"She'll get it, too, Steele!" Engles growled, as Angelo moved up beside the Virginian and reached out with both hands toward the Colt Hartford barrel.

"Reckon you people win," the Virginian drawled as he finally suppressed the self-anger that was triggered by the first sight of Engles and the initial touch of Newman's gun. He turned slightly from the waist to press the rifle barrel into the young Mexican's hands and released his hold on the stock and frame.

"It is our intention that all of us win, *señor*," Angelo said as he went down on to his haunches and drew the knife from the split seam in Steele's pants leg. "If you do as we ask, only the ogre Hernando Vettori will lose. His life."

"And you will do as we ask!" Martha Craig snapped, not as successful as the Virginian at controlling her rage.

"You can bet on it, punk!" Engles added viciously.

"I never do," Steele responded as the Mexican woman crumpled on the sidewalk uttered a strangled cry of terror.

"Never what?" Newman asked as Angelo stepped across in front of the Virginian.

"Bet on a long shot."

Chapter Six

"NO, ANGELO!" Martha Craig shrieked.

But her grandson was already committed to the action he had begun. The rifle and knife were in his left hand, so that it was his right which arced downward as he dropped into a half crouch, the palm crashing against Renita's cheek. The tone of the woman's cry altered from fear to agony as the force of the blow snapped her head around and slammed her temple onto the sidewalk.

"*Traidora!*" Angelo snarled, and used the rifle as a crutch to support himself on his lame right leg as he drew back the left to aim a kick at the woman's stomach.

Steele experienced an expansion of ice-cold anger now: directed at the brutal young Mexican. And felt his lips involuntarily curl back from his teeth and the skin draw tight between his cheekbones and jawline as he half turned and bent from the waist, both his gloved hands clawed. Newman's gun was no longer touching his flesh but he knew it was still aimed at him. As Engles grunted and swung the Smith and Wesson onto a new target.

His hands fastened around the raised ankle of Angelo. A moment before Newman's knee slammed into his crotch from behind.

He was sent into a crazy stagger, still bent over and holding the Mexican's leg. Air rushed out through his clenched teeth, carrying a moan of pain that was drowned under Angelo's shriek of alarm.

Engles and Mrs. Craig backed away. Steele lost his footing and fell forward, but managed to change direction as he jerked Angelo off his feet. The Mexican's cry became one of pain as he was slammed face down to the sidewalk, then rose in shrillness as the Virginian's weight collapsed on top of him.

"No!" Mrs. Craig commanded, and knocked Engles's gun hand to the side.

"Frig it!" the bounty hunter snarled, shoving the old woman away from him as he brought the small gun to bear again.

"She's right, Brad!" Newman snapped, an edge of anxiety to his voice as he saw his partner's fury rise to new heights at Martha Craig's intervention. "He's actin' the Southern gentleman is all."

Steele had been close to death on countless occasions. But in that part of a second as he looked up along the revolver barrel, the length of Engles's arm, and into the man's quivering face he knew this was the closest call he had ever had. And that his life depended on Newman's words finding some tiny receptive area within a mind otherwise filled with a rage too powerful to respond to outside influence.

The man's trigger finger gleamed white to either side of the guard. His eyes burned like pools of dark fire.

"Vettori, Bradley!" Martha Craig said, softly but very distinctly.

Newman had failed but the old woman succeeded. Engles continued to stare fixedly at the Virginian for perhaps two seconds, but his enlarged eyes narrowed.

"Sonofabitch," he muttered, the curse forcing his lips apart. Then he took a deep breath and offered: "Sorry, Dwight."

"Okay, old buddy," Newman acknowledged, relief evident in his voice. "Take care of the woman. Steele, get up off Angelo."

The young Mexican had frozen as solid as the Virginian, fearful of a shot that might miss Steele and hit him. Both men got slowly and painfully to their feet as the advancing form of Engles spurred Renita into fast movement. She was still afraid, the emotion contorting her beautiful face more than the flushed bruise on her cheek. Steele hid his response to a fresh source of pain behind impassiveness. Angelo looked ashamed.

"Right!" the moustached Newman snapped. "Now we're this close, we might as well get over to the Filbert Street place. All of us."

"I think that will be wise," Martha Craig agreed. "Renita, you and Adam Steele will walk ahead. We will be close behind. Both of you are now fully aware that if we are forced to abandon our assassination attempt, you will pay the price with your lives."

The younger woman refused to meet the steady gaze of the older one. Chose to ignore everybody except Steele, as she took short steps towards him and grasped his upper arm with tense, clawed fingers.

"I am sorry, Adam," she whispered. "I did not allow enough time. We should have waited until . . ."

"Move!" Newman ordered. "You know the way, Renita."

As they started forward, moving diagonally across Vallejo toward the corner of Davis Street, the Virginain showed the Mexican woman a boyish smile that more than countered his prematurely gray hair and seemed to take several years off his true age.

"You gave me a hand," he told her. "I played it wrong."

"You had bad luck, that is all, Adam Steele," Martha Craig said as she and the three men trailed the couple by a yard, Newman having to scrape his feet along the street to keep on his hurriedly donned and unlaced boots. "I recalled your request that the lamp should not be relit. And that worried me, since I was—and still am—certain you are a man who has a reason for everything. Then I remembered Angelo had cut one of your bonds so that you could eat and drink."

She paused and her tone took on an edge of bitterness. "It was our concern for the safety of Renita as much as fear of losing you which caused us to hurry back. Which was when our good fortune really shone. For we saw you approach before you saw us and were thus able to conceal ourselves."

"*Señora*, I intended no harm to you and the others. It is just that I have pity for Adam and . . ."

"Shut your stinkin' mouth, bitch!" Engles snarled.

The woman trembled and dug her fingers harder into the Virginian's upper arm.

"Easy," he soothed.

"Cut the talk, all of you!" Newman growled, and lowered his own voice to rasping whisper. "This area of the city may look like a ghost town, but it ain't."

"Dwight is correct," Mrs. Craig added. "Earlier we were asked twice by men if we had seen somebody answering your description, Adam Steele. It seems that the whore you killed was very highly regarded at the Havelock Hotel.

69

The owners have posted a five thousand-dollar reward for your capture and the news of this has traveled fast."

"*Si, señor,*" Angelo said, still humble after his display of cowardly brutality toward his countrywoman. "You are fortunate we caught you again. There are many men in this city who would be happy to shoot you on sight for even half that reward."

"You want me to be grateful, feller?" Steele asked.

"I said to all be quiet!" Newman reminded tensely.

The Virginian felt the way the bounty hunter sounded but neither his face nor his voice revealed anything stronger than nonchalance as he said: "You want to stop and see if we can hear what we thought we saw?"

"Do that," Newman came back quickly.

"What is it?" the old woman asked as the younger one swallowed hard.

"Up the street, look and listen," Newman urged, his words no more than pin drops through the silence that closed around the group as they halted.

They had turned the corner and were two blocks up Battery Street from Vallejo. There were buildings on the west side of the street, facing out onto vacant lots where other buildings had been torn down. The mist off the bay which curled around and over the tops of the buildings on Front Street seemed to swirl faster

70

and grow thicker as it rolled across the rubble-littered open area.

It was at the very limit of visibility—perhaps fifty yards up and across the street—that the Virginian had glimpsed two blurred shapes that appeared to have human form. Had Dwight Newman not spoken so tautly, Steele might have set aside his suspicion, for the constantly moving mist caused the heaps of burned timber and smashed masonry to assume many odd shapes. But he respected the judgment of a man whose natural instincts for danger had allowed him to survive the experience of bounty hunting in Mexico.

"I don't see nothin'," Engles growled truculently.

"How many times you said that and been wrong?" his partner countered sourly. "To the right, a hundred and fifty feet or so, Steele?"

"That's it."

"How many?"

"Reckon I saw two."

"Check."

"And they've seen us, feller."

"Yeah, or they wouldn't have ducked outta sight."

"We are in your hands, Dwight," Martha Craig said. "What do you suggest?"

"Start walkin' again. Like we decided we didn't see them after all. Angelo, carry that rifle at the slope. Brad, you and me'll close up on Steele and Renita so those jokers don't see our

71

guns. Steele, if it looks like trouble, go down to the left. Take her with you. Martha and Angelo, you see Steele make that move, you hit the street fast. Right, move."

No word had been spoken above a harsh whisper. The sounds of footfalls on the sidewalk seemed disproportionately loud. Sweat moistened flesh as the mist dampened clothing. The two men at the edge of the vacant lot used the cover of the mist and the sound of the group's advance to cross the street. When they took form out of the moon-tinged mist they were staggering, each with an arm around the other's shoulder: going through the charade of being drunk. Their free hands waved in the air to either side. And they did not lift their eyes from the ground until they were only twenty feet away from the group of captors and captives.

Neither Steele nor Newman could be sure these were the men they had glimpsed briefly on the other side of the street a minute or so earlier. But both were certain that the men were not liquored up as much as they pretended to be. For their youthful complexions were not flushed and the whites of their eyes showed not a trace of bloodshot. They were dressed like seamen, in soft-soled boots, dirty white denim pants, high-necked black jerseys, and head-hugging woollen hats.

One of them executed a good imitation of a drunk's slack-mouthed grin as Steele came to a halt, pulling Renita up short at his side and forcing the three men and the old woman to stop behind him.

The other stranger slurred: "Say, we headin' right for the Barbary Coast?"

The Virginian distrusted the gap between the two men which meant that neither could reach completely over the shoulder of the other: keeping a right and a left hand out of sight. He had to trust the reflexes of Newman and Engles.

He made his move the instant the pressure of the older bounty hunter's gun was removed from the small of his back. Without giving any warning of his intent, he powered to the side. The woman gave vent to both fear and pain as his hip bone crashed against hers and sent her hard to the sidewalk. As he fell after her, he screwed his head to the side to watch the fake drunks. Saw them come abruptly upright and drag their concealed hands into sight, fisted around the butts of Colt .45s.

Newman and Engles took no chances. Operated a plan they had obviously used many times before. The first shots erupted dark stains on the seamen's jerseys and sent them staggering backward, shock and pain inscribed in their faces. Two more pairs of shots exploded, resounding off the façades of the buildings and then fading away into the mist. Other patches of blood expanded across the strangers' jerseys as they dropped their guns, leaned against each other, then corkscrewed into a single heap on the sidewalk.

Steele craned his neck around still further and saw both the bounty hunters in identical attitudes. The gunfighter's stance of a half crouch, sideways to the enemy. The forefingers of their right hands were hooked tightly to the triggers of the Smith and Wessons. Their left hands were held just above the guns, the heels poised to fan at the hammers again if it were necessary.

But it was not.

The seaman who had asked the question was dead before he hit the ground. The other one coughed and the rush of air from his lungs spilled blood out over his lips. Then he lay still. Both died with their eyes wide open and the expression they suggested was of pained disappointment.

"Hey, we still got what it takes, old buddy!" Brad Engles exclaimed excitedly.

"We sure have, partner," Newman agreed with a sigh of pride and satisfaction in a job well done.

Steele got to his feet and stooped to help the trembling woman stand up. Martha Craig was also badly shaken and had to lean against a building front after her grandson had lifted her gently from the sidewalk. She seemed unable to wrench her staring eyes away from the crumpled and bullet-riddled corpses. Only succeeded by raising both thin hands to her emaciated face and blocking off the view.

"How terrible," she said hoarsely between the inverted V of her wrists as she swung to put her back to the bodies.

"No time for that, Martha," Newman snapped. "We got to get away from here before people come to check on the shootin'."

"Yeah, Steele!" the now delighted Engles growled. "Move your own and that bitch's ass outta here. You did fine just then. Keep it that way and I figure we got us an unbeatable team."

"Brad's right," Newman agreed, grinning as he gestured with his gun for Steele and Renita to move around the inert bodies slumped on the sidewalk. "You did real good."

"Adam, do not let them praise you into doing as they wish," the woman at his side urged the Virginian, staring intently into his hard, moonlit profile.

"Don't worry about that," he muttered sourly with a bleak glance down at the corpses. "I've just seen what kind of fans they are."

Chapter Seven

THE TWO seamen had been gunned down in a commercial area of the city. Nobody lived close by and if the shooting was overheard from a distance the group of four men and two women were well clear before the cautiously curious reached the scene.

At first Steel, Renita, Newman, and Engles were far ahead of Angelo and Martha Craig: the grandson anxiously trying to impart the need for haste to his grandmother. But not until the bodies were veiled by mist and then hidden by intervening buildings when a corner was turned, did the old woman recover from the shock of witnessing the violent killings. The young Mexican was able to get through to her then and they hurried to catch up, rejoining the main group just a few yards short of Filbert Street.

"I apologize, Dwight," Mrs. Craig said humbly, "for my behavior. But I have never seen anyone shot down in front of my very eyes."

"Never mind, ma'am," Steele offered as Renita steered him around a corner and they started down a street which dead-ended at a pair of high iron gates. "It's good practice for watching what happens to Hernando Vettori."

"Shut your mouth," Newman ordered.

"No, he is right," the old woman countered. "All things are relative, Adam Steele. I have just witnessed the horror of two innocent men dying violently. And it will help me to keep a grip on myself when I see Vettori die. For I will have in my mind a more vivid image than ever of the greater carnage for which that monster is responsible."

Newman vented a short laugh. "You just can't win, can you, Steele?" he crowed.

"Always say a man has to take the rough with the smooth," the Virginian responded evenly as they halted briefly in front of the gates.

Angelo had a key which fitted the padlocked chain that secured the gates and he used it again to refasten them after the group had gone through onto a long, broad area behind a row of warehouses. The surface beneath their feet was cement, ridged by the lines and ties of three railroad sidings. The metal was rusty and the cement was cracked and holed. The warehouse the group approached was the middle one of three that had a disused and decayed aura in the mist-filtered moonlight. To the right, the railroad lines gleamed and the warehouses had a fresher and more lively look about them. A string of boxcars stood on one of the sidings, half loaded with wooden crates when the day's work was complete. Several crates had been left standing in the open between the rear doors of the warehouse and the freight train when the roustabouts went home.

Angelo had stayed ahead of the group beyond the gates and now used another key to open a small door at the corner of one of the abandoned and derelict buildings. Like those flanking it, it was about a hundred feet wide, towered to the height of a three-story building, and stretched at least two hundred feet toward the dock and piers at the edge of the bay. Beyond this, mist and shadowy night blocked the Virginian's view. It was built of timber and had a flat roof.

"See that train of boxcars, Steele?" Newman asked as the young Mexican had some trouble with the door lock.

"Sure, feller."

"They'll hitch a locomotive to it tomorrow and she'll pull out at noon. But there'll be another freight train being loaded on the next track before then. Won't leave until five. Bound for Omaha. Up to you where you get off."

"Easy as that?" Steele said wryly.

"For you," Newman answered gruffly. "Wasn't easy for us to set up. The brakeman on your train drives a hard bargain."

The Virginian pursed his lips. "We all have our problems."

"Will you let me go with him, please?" Renita asked miserably as Angelo was finally able to turn the key in the lock.

"We didn't make no travel plans for you, bitch!" Engles growled.

"How could we know you needed any?" Angelo hissed over his shoulder as he pushed open the door.

"No dice," Newman told her coldly and waved his gun to gesture them into the warehouse. "We'll think of somethin' else to do with a sneaky lady like you."

She vented a low, choked cry and brought her free arm up to grip Steele with two hands, pressing the side of her body tightly against his. In the pitch darkness of the warehouse after the door was closed, Newman or Engles also moved close to the Virginian. And he felt the cold, mist-moist ring of a gun muzzle on the flesh of his neck again. He also felt something else: but for the first time. A faint stirring of sexual want for the beautiful and afraid woman at his side.

But he forced cold reason into his mind before vivid lustful images could crowd it. Ever since the naked whore had fled from her room at the Havelock Hotel, it was as if he had entered into a world of unreality set just below the level of the actual. The escape of the gray-bearded killer as the Oriental woman used her dying breath to accuse the wrong man of murdering her. The chase through the crowded and empty streets of the city. The capture in the spice-smelling warehouse. The story of the brutal massacre in far-off Mexico years ago. The strange assortment of people who formed the desperate group bent on assassinating the former *Federale* officer. The way that Renita had aided his escape. The ambush and recapture. The killing of the two seamen.

The recollections came quickly and smoothly into Steele's mind: in strict chronological order. And his mind's eye viewed every recent event with stark clarity. None of them, in his memory, as clouded by the ocean mist or the blurring effect of concussion which had been present at the time they took place. Only Steele himself, and his responses to the actions of others, appeared to be surrounded by whirling haze. A figure central to everything that had occurred, and yet taking little part in directing the events.

Which was not his way: and this is what gave his world since early evening the air of unreality.

And just before a match flared, and the light expanded as the flame was touched to a lamp wick, a crazy idea brought this process of thought to an end. Darkness and light. Passive negative and a positive emotional response. But would the taking of the Mexican woman in such circumstances act as a first step back toward the reality of being the kind of man he had become since the early days of the War Between the States? Or would he simply be indulging in just one more fantasy?

"Steele," Engles said, announcing himself as the one who had held the revolver against the Virginian's flesh.

Steele turned and Renita tried to retain her double-handed grip on him. But then she screamed as Angelo hooked an arm around her waist and wrenched her away. At precisely the same moment as Newman stepped up close to Steele's back, thrust his arms under the smaller man's armpits and interlocked his fingers at the nape of the neck.

The Virginian formed his teeth and lips to utter a mild curse as he was locked tight against the arched-forward body of Newman. Glimpsed Renita being dragged away from him by the grim-faced Angelo, a placid Martha Craig in the process of setting down the newly lit lamp on the floor, and the brutally grinning features of Brad Engles.

The bounty hunter's right hand was drawn out from under his jacket lapel, formed into a fist that was no longer around the butt of the .38.

"To teach you a friggin' lesson, punk!" the man rasped through his clenched, tobacco-stained teeth. And used his knee while he pulled back his right arm for a full-blooded punch.

The knee slammed into Steele's crotch at the front—to release a bolt of agony far more intense than the kick Newman had delivered earlier at the back.

The curse Steele had intended to voice emerged as a groan: cut short as the bounty hunter's fist smashed into his mouth. He tasted the saltiness and warmth of flowing blood on the roof of his mouth. His eyes stung with the saline smartness of involuntary tears.

"Be careful of his arms and hands, Dwight," Martha Craig warned dully, as if she knew full wall it was unnecessary to caution Newman. Her tone was sharper and firmer when she said: "And you take care not to injure his eyesight, Bradley."

The Virginian blinked and shook his head. The people to each side and in front of him were blurred, the way his own image had been as he recalled the series of events since Lotus Blossom's left breast took a bullet wound. Their backdrop, lit from below by the kerosene lamp on the floor, showed in sharp focus.

A high, wide, dark cavern of a place. Cement floor littered with torn paper sacks and discarded pieces of timber. Walls stained by damp and featured with tightly boarded windows. Iron pillars rising up through the darkness to support a roof he could not see. Lengths of frayed rope hanging down out of the darkness. An unrailed stairway canting up one wall.

"You are stupid!" Renita shrieked. "Spite will achieve nothing."

A hand struck flesh and Steele felt no pain. He heard the woman scream.

A short burst of Spanish from Angelo.

He smelled the damp and decay of the derelict surroundings.

A searing explosion erupted in his belly as Engles landed another punch.

Burning kerosene permeated the dank atmosphere. Then a sharp, more acrid smell. He blinked again and saw that the younger bounty hunter had a glowing cheroot clenched between his grinning teeth.

"You hear me, punk? This is what you get for tryin' to cross us! Try it again and you'll really get it bad! We won't kill you, you little runt!"

He leaned forward and launched a right cross and a left jab. The first blow caught Steele on the side of the jaw and rocked his head far to the left. The second punished again the Virginian's belly.

"You know what we'll do? We'll break every lousy finger of both your hands. Then we'll turn you loose on the streets. So you'll be a sittin' duck for every barfly and saloon drunk who's heard about the reward on your stinkin' head!"

Renita screamed again. Steele was not sure if

84

he had heard Angelo hit her. And he did not have the energy to screw his head around to look at her. Newman seemed to be applying more pressure, forcing his shoulders up and his head down. A point at the top of his spine felt as if it was taking more punishment than his face and his belly under the assaults of Engles.

"But that is purely academic, Adam Steele," Martha Craig said, and she sounded as close to him at the front as Newman was at the back.

His hat was knocked off his head and then a hank of his hair was clutched in a tight fist. His chin was jerked up off his chest and he was forced to look into the old woman's emaciated face over a range of less than twelve inches. Her gray, age-mottled skin was cut with a countless number of lines. He could still detect a faint trace of chili on her hot breath.

"You will have no further opportunity to escape. In a few moments you will be taken upstairs and locked in the room we have arranged for you. A room you will now share with the slut who has betrayed us. You can minister to each other's injuries. Do anything you like, except escape. Because the room will be guarded every moment until you are brought out to undertake the execution of Hernando Vettori."

She released her grip on his hair and stepped back. It took an enormous effort for Steele to hold his head erect unaided, and to look into

Martha Craig's face as it expressed a mixture of disappointment and contrition.

"I am extremely sorry, Adam Steele. I had hoped to convince you with the facts that we deserve to succeed in our aim. If that failed, then I assumed such a man as you would be eager to work for the money we have offered. Force is our last resort."

She shook her head and moved to the side, to allow Engles access to the helpless Virginian. "Just sufficient to compose him so that we may get him upstairs, Bradley."

Steele was aware of blood in his mouth and running out over his lower lip. The whole area of his shoulders and neck where the silent Newman gripped him had become numb. His belly was on fire. He could not feel the floor beneath his feet.

"No trouble, Mrs. Craig," the grinning Engles replied, the words floating out on a long stream of blue tobacco smoke.

He used his knee again and Steele tasted bile with the blood in his mouth. He swallowed hard and screwed his eyes shut. Another right cross slammed into his jaw and a tooth punctured flesh again to spurt fresh blood against his palate.

He struggled to detach his mind from his physical being: tried to drag it up out of the sea of pain by searching for reason to explain the group's new tactic. For it made no sense at all. But perhaps there was no sense to it. Maybe desperation had driven them to this extreme of spite, pure and simple.

"Not enough, my dear," he heard Mrs. Craig say, her voice forcing him back to sharp awareness of his suffering.

He tensed himself for more blows. But the punches which hit flesh were not aimed at him. The Mexican woman who a few minutes earlier had aroused sexual want in him screamed and screamed again.

"That's it, Angelo. Mark her badly, my dear. So that she will recall for a long time how wrong it was of her to betray us."

Then two punches slammed into the Virginian's stomach. He felt his mouth snap open and heard the air rush out. He opened his eyes briefly as his head fell forward, and saw specks of bright crimson become larger and darker as they soaked into the blue material of his suit jacket.

"Figure that's softened him up enough, old buddy."

The pressure was relieved from his shoulders and neck. He experienced the sensation of falling a long way for a long time. But he no longer trusted time. He heard the thud of his limp form hitting the cement floor but he did not feel any pain at the impact.

"Be as easy to handle as a day-old babe, Brad."

He had collapsed into a heap. Was aware of being rolled onto his back.

"But a little heavier, Dwight. Here, you take his arms. I'll grab his feet."

He was lifted up off the floor and the timing seemed right now: it was sound that could not be relied upon. The voices of the two bounty hunters had a gentle tone to his ears and seemed to float down to him from high in the darkness beyond the reach of the lamplight.

If they bumped him against anything carrying him up the stairway, he did not feel it. He was back in a fantasy world again, seemingly wrapped in a warm cocoon that protected him from anything that was harmful or evil. It was like being caught in suspended animation on the narrow dividing line between waking and sleeping. And after he had been put down and heard the footfalls of Newman and Engles recede into infinity he waited eagerly for sleep to engulf him.

But it would not come. More footfalls approached him. There was a dull thud and a soft curse. The footsteps went back to where they had come from.

The sound of a door being slammed was very real. And triggered stark reality within Steele.

In a split second the cocoon was ripped from around him and his every nerve ending screamed for relief from suffering. His awareness demanded a vocal outlet for the agony, but anger rose first into his throat and constricted it.

"*Madre de Dios!*" Renita gasped. "I hate

them more than Hernando Vettori!" She caught her breath. "Adam? Adam, are you all right?"

He was grateful for her presence. That she was conscious, able to speak and move. For he could force his mind to concentrate on something outside his own punished self. The abstract would not have been sufficient, as it had been when the beating had ended. For the waves of pain that washed over him were too powerful. And even now he had to fool himself into being convinced that it was vitally important to get a fix on the woman. To judge exactly where she was in relation to him, and the rate at which she was inching painfully toward him.

"Please answer me, Adam. Please tell me you are here with me. I am so afraid."

He tried to reply, but rage—hotter even than his agony—refused to open his throat for anything other than damp, sea-smelling air.

The words she spoke gave him the direction he was looking for. The woman was over to the left, down on the floor with him. Would probably take fifteen seconds to reach him.

"I'll kill the whole frigging lot of the bastards!"

Anger had beaten pain to find an outlet. The words emerged with the power of a roar but sounded in his ears at the level and tone of a harsh whisper. A tiny section of his mind experienced surprise at the uncharacteristic use of strong language.

"Ah, you are here with me," Renita breathed. "And you are awake."

"And I reckon to stay that way," he rasped. "Don't ever again intend to be caught napping."

Chapter Eight

IN THE pitch darkness of his second windowless prison cell, Steele could do no more than
voice his protests as the young Mexican woman
stripped him naked and eased him up off the
bare floorboards and onto the relative softness
of two folded blankets. She offered no argu-
ment, and only spoke to whisper a soft-voiced
apology whenever a move she eased upon him
triggered a groan of pain from him.

Soon, he became as silent as she, until she began to bathe his bruised face and belly with
cool water. Then, from time to time, he sighed
his relief as her gentle ministrations took the
sharp edges off his suffering.

"You are feeling a little better now, Adam?"
she asked softly after a long time had passed.

So softly that he probably would not have

heard the words had she not trailed her fingers over his bruised jaw and cut lips as she spoke. Because as he lay quietly on the blankets and felt the level of pain subside, resting and relishing the touch of her hands and the water, he drifted close to the edge of a peaceful, natural sleep.

Now he snapped open his eyes to the darkness that was as full as that behind his lids. And had to delve deep into his mind to recall what the Mexican woman had said to him.

"Almost good, Renita," he replied. "I'm grateful to you."

"I am glad."

Her fingers moved away from his face and he felt the brush of her hair on his bare chest. Then the pressure of the side of her face against his flesh, which drew a response far beyond the point of contact.

"I am glad about something else, too."

The Virginian continued to lie absolutely still and it was not fear of triggering fresh waves of pain from his injuries which caused him to do this. He was naked, enclosed within the privacy of total darkness with a desirable woman. A woman who had made it known she was attracted to him the first time they saw each other. A woman who had reason to be as grateful to him as he was to her. So he forced himself to remain unmoving because he was afraid he would be unable to control the emotions she was stirring within him. Emotions he felt quite capable of indulging in the state of near euphoria which had gripped him as the effects of the beating became less intense.

"What's that?" To his own ears his voice sounded hoarse.

"That I was ashamed and am no longer so. Because you feel as I do. Which perhaps means that we can share some happiness in this terrible time."

She moved, lifting her head from his chest as she wriggled the length of her body to press it against his. Her lips were close to his ear. One of her hands began again to trail its fingers over his face. The other explored his hirsute chest for long moments. Then, as she whispered to him, its fingertips traveled across smooth, hard-packed flesh.

"Please prove I am right, Adam. Do not make me feel shame again. While I bathed you it was necessary to touch you. Here. And here."

She vented a sound that was half sigh, half laugh—powering a fierce draught of hot breath into his ear—as her fingers moved gently on the flesh at his crotch, then closed into a fist around it.

"I was thinking only of you, *mi amor*. I wanted only to ease your pain. But I am a woman and I cannot help the feelings I experience. I tried, Adam. I told myself you were too sick. That even if you were not, you have no feeling for me. That even if there was such a feeling, we must give all our time to thinking of a way out of the trouble we are in."

Again the odd sound burst from her lips. But the expelled breath that exploded against his ear was almost cool in comparison with the heat of her hand enclosing his throbbing flesh.

"I reckon we have time, Renita," Steele told her, his voice still thick. "And we've both got the inclination. But I'm not sure I can stand the pace."

The hand on his face moved to press two fingers to his swollen lips.

"*Cállate, mi amor*," she whispered. "Lie still, Adam."

Her hands and body moved away from him and she stood up. Steele widened his eyes to their fullest extent but he could not penetrate the darkness which was suddenly filled with soft sounds. His own and the woman's breathing and the rustle of fabric on fabric—then on flesh.

A sense of the unreal closed in around the Virginian again and for stretched seconds he was convinced that he was dreaming. But then this conviction was driven from his mind as Renita knelt down at this side and caught her breath, brushing his thighs as she swung a leg to straddle him. Steele also held his breath and both together the air was expelled from their lungs as she lowered herself down on top of him. The centers of their wants met and mingled. The distended nipples of her breasts touched his chest. Droplets of sweat dripped from her flesh to his. Her hair fell across his face. Her lips uttered soft Mexican words as they moved on his neck and throat. Her back arched and sagged.

Steele sighed his pleasure, then had to choke back a groan of pain as the want he felt involuntarily raised his back off the blankets to meet the downward movement of the woman's body.

"Be still, Adam," Renita murmured. "I will know when it is time. Trust me, *mi amor*."

He raised his hands and was able to ignore the pain this triggered from his shoulders: trade it with pleasure as he cupped the inverted cones of her breasts.

The rise and fall of her body increased in pace as her passion heightened by the same degree his did.

He moved his hands again, away from her body to her head. Her hair was silken to his touch, her flesh soft and firm in its molding to her bone structure. As he explored the rises and indentations from her forehead down to her eyes he could visualize her beautiful features.

Then his fingertips traveled over her cheeks and mouth and jaw. And he felt the rock-hard contusions Angelo's fists had raised on her face: here and there discovered the ridges of congealed blood where the force of the blows had broken the skin.

Just for a moment he was on the point of

pushing her away as he realized she had tended his injuries and ignored her own. But the intensity of her desire for satisfaction abruptly increased. She started to gasp for breath and her sweat-dripping body pumped harder and faster upon his. The moans that burst from her trembling lips were far removed from those of suffering. And these signs of her passionate need blotted from his mind everything except his own lust to complete the act.

So instead of interrupting her, he returned his hands to her hair, grasping the strands in his fists and grinding her face harder into his neck as he raised his head and sucked at her flesh.

She shuddered through orgasm, but was not content with her own release: kept up the frenetic rise and fall of her satiated body until she felt the man beneath her spend himself. Only then sank limply to press the entire length of herself against him.

"Adam, Adam," she murmured. "It has been so long. Thank you, *mi amor*. Please do not hate me."

Abruptly, she was gentle again. Easing herself up from him and then rolling off his body, to sprawl onto her back on the bare boards of the floor. She filled her lungs with air, held it for a long time and hissed it out through clenched teeth.

"Hate you?" he asked huskily.

"For making such demands on you after what that *bastardo* Engles did to you."

"Something I say a lot, Renita," he told her, stretching out a hand to cup one of her breasts, then running it down the sweat-slick length of her body to linger briefly in the tangle of moist hair at the base of her belly. "A man has to take the rough with the smooth. Maybe I never knew exactly what that meant before tonight."

She did not reply for long moments. Then called through the darkness, as he withdrew his hand and she reached out to clutch it. "Adam?"

"Yes."

"I think I love you. After these few short hours, I believe that I do."

He took his hand away from her grasp, then used both arms to lever himself up into a sitting posture. The action completely dispelled the feeling of well-being that had followed his climax, by swamping it with fresh waves of pain from his shoulders and the pit of his stomach.

"How do you think of me, Adam?"

"Right now," he rasped through gritted teeth, "I think you're crazy."

"Both of us are, I think."

"No, not for what you did, Renita," he corrected, and had to interrupt himself as he devoted his whole attention to the process of getting shakily to his feet. "If you could bottle it you might advance the cause of medical science a million years. I mean crazy for spending all your time patching me up without taking care of yourself."

She surprised him then, by rasping a Mexican

obscenity he understood. She seemed to sense the effect it had on him and as she stood up, she said: "I am sorry, Adam. But what Angelo did to me was as nothing to the way you were beaten. Please be careful, *mi amor*."

This last she said anxiously as he took his first couple of steps, and had to hook a hand over her naked shoulder to keep from falling.

"Tell me about this place," he instructed as he released his grip on her and began to take short steps unaided—hands out in front of him to guard against banging into obstacles.

"It is a warehouse on the waterfront. Not used for many years. Soon to be pulled down with its neighbors when they will be replaced by a building for the authorities who run the port. It is the company Señora Craig inherited from her dead husband which is to make these alterations. Which is why we—they!—have been able to come here. It is the same construction company which will also rebuild that section of Vallejo Street where you were brought first of all."

"She's a rich lady, uh?" The initial agony of moving about had passed and now the Virginian was able to part his teeth as well as his lips as he spoke.

"Very rich, I think. But very mean. She lives frugally in a large mansion beside the ocean. And would contribute no more than the rest of us to the payment we offered you. But it would have made no difference, would it, Adam? If

98

she had promised you one million American dollars you would not shoot Hernando Vettori, I think."

Steele explored the room and its furnishings as he attempted to walk off the disabling effects of his pain. And discovered a crude wooden bed from which the woman had removed the blankets, a chair, and a table. On the table was an empty pitcher and a basin half full with water.

He gathered up his clothes and sat on the edge of the bed to dress. Guessing what he was doing from the sounds he made, Renita also began to put on her clothes.

"What makes you so sure?" he asked.

"I am a woman. So is Señora Craig, but for many weeks now she has been concerned with only one thing. So it has been impossible for her to think as a normal woman. But I am not so single-minded as she. As all of them. When I first saw you, I knew they had chosen the wrong man. Something told me this."

"Feminine intuition," Steele put in.

"I do not know what it is called. I do know I could not have lain with you as I did if you were such a man. For a long time, whenever Newman came to Guerrero, he tried to possess me. But I could not allow such as he to touch me without a feeling of revulsion."

"Somebody did more than touch you, Renita."

There was a tense pause and as Steele hung

the weighted scarf around his neck he expected her to vent anger. But she merely sighed softly before she answered.

"I have said I love you and asked how you feel for me, Adam. You have a right to know of this. There was a man in Guerrero. The son of the storekeeper. If Vettori had not come to the village, perhaps José and I would now be married."

"He wasn't one of the wounded?"

"No. He was shot dead by the *Federales*. And because of that I had always wished to see Hernando Vettori die. But since I saw you carried into the condemned house by Newman and Engles, it has ceased to have importance for me. I now wish only that . . . well, I think you know."

The Virginian was grateful to her for treating his injuries and had enjoyed emptying his need into her willing body. Anything else he felt for her was academic, since it rested in the future. The present pressed other considerations on him.

"Finish telling me about this place, Renita," he reminded softly.

"Of course. Right now I am less important than this trouble you are in. This room is in the loft at the back of the building. It was once the place where the document work for the loading and unloading of ships was done. At the front of the building there is a hatchway where there used to be machinery for lifting heavy objects. From the hatchway there is a good view across the dock and along the pier where Vettori's ship will tie up. It is from there that they intend for you to shoot him. If you had done this, you would then have been able to jump down onto some bales of hay, run to the rear door of the warehouse and then to the train outside."

"The only doors are at the front and rear?"

"*Si*. Big doors that slide but these are locked and there are no keys. Angelo has the key that unlocks the door through which we came."

"Windows?"

"Many, but all are boarded up so that not a chink of light comes in or gets out. For they plan to remain here until Vettori gets off his ship. And some of the men who work on the waterfront start before dawn. So if one of them saw a light from this place it might lead to the murder plot being discovered."

After he dressed, Steele had felt his way to a wall and started to move carefully around the extent of the converted office. It was some hundred feet square, with tightly boarded windows on two sides. The only door had no handle or keyhole. When he pressed his ear against the panel, he heard nothing.

"They hoped they would not need to use this room, Adam," Renita went on. "You were taken to the house first because people were still working close by this place. This room was prepared in case you proved difficult. But it would have been better for them if there was no need to keep you a prisoner."

Steele moved away from the door. "They brought you up here after me."

"*Si.*"

"Said downstairs they planned to guard us. Do you know who's standing sentry duty?"

"Angelo dragged me here. Newman and Engles were outside. I heard the bolts being moved across the door. I did not hear anyone going away. Perhaps all of them are out there."

He clicked his tongue against the roof of his mouth. "We'll never know unless we can get the door open."

"How?" Her fear could be heard in just this single word. Was emphasized when she added, "It is very strong and there are three bolts, Adam."

"I'm going to curl up on the floor. Make some noises like I'm very sick. Want you to bang on the door and tell whoever's out there you think Engles overdid the beating. That I could be dying from the pounding my stomach took."

"But what if there is more than one, Adam? Or if just one, he might call the others before he opens the door. Engles said . . ."

"A lot of things," Steele cut in as his punished body welcomed the rest when he lowered himself to the folded blankets and rolled onto his side, pulling his knees up against his chest.

"They need me too much to kill me, except as a last resort. Just do as I told you."

"All right. You are ready?"

"Whenever you are."

Even the rustle of her dresss fabric against her flesh had a sound of fear to it as the woman moved cautiously toward the door. On the way, she bumped against the table and the metal pitcher clanged the metal basin.

"Angelo!" she called. "Dwight Newman! Engles! Whoever is there, you had better come in!"

She had no need to feign anxiety as she thudded her fist on the door panel.

"Can you hear me? Is anyone there? Please, Adam is in great pain!"

"Shut up, bitch!" It was Bradley Engles who snarled the response and the prospect of this man entering the room alone caused Steele to curl his lip away from his teeth to show to the darkness a brutal grin of evil anticipation.

"Please listen to me!" the woman insisted. "You have hit him too hard, I think! He cannot walk or even get up! There is great pain in his stomach! If there is not help for him, I think he may die!"

"Die?" Engles growled. "Friggin' hell!"

"You will please come to see!"

There was a long silence during which both the Virginian and Renita held their breath.

Then Engles rasped: "Okay, I'm comin' in! But this better not be a lousy trick! Both of you be where I can see you! If you ain't, I'll start blastin'!"

There was another silence. Then the scraping of bolts through brackets.

Renita spoke a few words in her native tongue and Steele guessed she was saying a prayer. He began to voice low groans and to move this way and that on the blanket, clutching his stomach with both hands. His back was to the door but he was aware of it opening: for his eyes were not quite closed and he saw light enter the room and brighten as the door swung on its oiled hinges. He began to give voice to a harsh agony he no longer felt, kneading his stomach with clawed hands: pushing his legs out straight and bringing them up again.

"Stand back there in the corner, bitch!" Engles snarled.

Between his moans, Steele heard the woman's bare feet slapping the floorboards as she complied with the order. Then the louder footfalls of the bounty hunter as he entered the room. The light source remained outside.

"Come on, punk, I didn't beat up on you that hard!"

Through the cracked lids of his eyes the Virginian saw Engles's shadow on the floor and wall. And put a shrill note into his groan as the man's boot nudged him in the small of the back. Then he spread his face with an expression to match the sounds he was making and rolled over on to his back.

The tall bounty hunter towered above him and did not back away, arrogantly confident as he aimed the Smith and Wesson revolver down at the face of Steele.

"I'm bleeding inside, Engles," the Virginian forced out through clenched teeth. "I can feel it." He groaned and jerked his back off the floor and his knees up to his chest. "Like there's something gnawing at my belly. I need a doctor, fast!"

"Si, Adam needs a doctor," Renita agreed anxiously from the corner where she cowered.

Steele had screwed his eyes tightly closed. Now he cracked them open to look up at the bounty hunter: saw a frown of concern on the hard, weathered face.

"I'll have Dwight and the old biddy check you out!" he said. And started to back away.

A genuine cry of searing agony burst from Steele's lips as he powered into another jerky movement. And perhaps would have died had not Engles snapped his head around to look toward a sound at his back.

The sound was made by the woman as she lunged out of the corner, snatching the empty pitcher from behind her back and gripping it in both hands to thrust above her head.

"Oh, Christ!" Engles blurted.

Steele rolled onto his side and swung his legs around behind the bounty hunter's heels, at the same moment shooting up his left hand to fasten a fist around the wrist of the man's gun hand. He twisted the wrist to divert the aim of the small revolver. And hauled himself half up on it, as he forced his thighs hard against the backs of Engles's calves.

His punished body signaled new protests of pain to his brain and he was gripped by a terrible depression as he felt the well of his energy drain out of him.

Bradley Engles would not fall: stood redwood straight and tall and seemed to express a patronizing grin as he forced his wrist around to bring the Smith and Wesson to bear on the sweat-run face of the weakened man below him.

But it was not any kind of grin he showed: except in the blurred vision of the Virginian. Rather, it was an expression of panic as the bounty hunter was torn between countering two attacks.

He misjudged the situation. Decided Steele had enough strength left to be the main danger. Thought he could deal with the Virginian and still have time to duck and whirl before Renita reached him.

But the woman's speed beat him and panic gripped his mind as he sensed her immediately behind him just as Steele's last reserve of strength was exhausted. He heard the pitcher swishing through the air and tried to jerk away from it. But Steele was still curled around his lower legs. The hollow metal slammed against the side of his head and he gasped a response as he started to fall.

Steele sucked air into his lungs and shook his head to shift the involuntary tears of pain from his eyes.

The gun dropped from Engles's open hand and thudded to the folded blankets. The Virginian ignored it for he was already clutching a weapon before the revolver bounced and came to rest.

He rasped soft words of encouragement to himself as he forced his back up off the floor again, snatching the scarf from around his neck by one of the weighted corners.

Engles was merely stunned by the blow with the pitcher. Or that was how it seemed to Steele as the bounty hunter turned in his fall and pushed out his hands to soften the impact with the floor. So he did not trust the stillness of the man's form as it lay prone, head screwed around and eyes closed.

"Adam!" Renita blurted in a harsh whisper.

Steele ignored the call as he forced himself up into a kneeling position: then flung himself along the length of Engles's body.

The impact of the Virginian on his back panicked the bounty hunter out of his pretense of unconsciousness. His eyes snapped open and he forced his head up off the floor and craned his neck even further to look at his attacker. For a split second, something gray like a tendril of

San Francisco ocean mist moved in front of his eyes. Then something with more substance than vapor curled around his neck. A cry of fear formed deep inside him, but a vicious constriction of his throat prevented its escape.

And it was the Virginian who uttered a sound. An animalistic grunt of joy as he caught the free-swinging weighted corner of the thuggee scarf and crossed his arms in front of his chest. The smell of triumph was crowding his nostrils and from this he drew fresh strength which seemed to fill and overflow the reservoir that only moments before had been drained.

He forced his back to straighten and spread his thighs to straddle the man who was at his mercy. This lifted Engles's head and chest off the floor.

"Adam, don't!" Renita implored.

He glanced to the side and saw her. The small revolver was in her hand. Her face, its beauty already marred by the bruises and torn skin of the beating, now became scarred by the ugliness of pure horror.

The Virginian felt a deep need to explain his actions to her. But this was not so powerful as the desire to kill Bradley Engles and to relish the emotional stimulus of the act.

So he shifted his dark, coldly staring eyes back to the bounty hunter's tortured profile. Saw the dying man's right eye expressing a pathetic, tacit plea toward the woman as his lips moved to form the three syllables of her name.

As his clawed hands made vain efforts to hook between the constricting fabric of the scarf and the leathery, bristled flesh that bulged above it.

Steele forced his own hands further apart, locking the elbow of his right arm into the half-folded joint of the left. And curled back his lips to show a cold grin of evil pleasure as Engles's mouth gaped wide and the man's eyelids stretched to their fullest extent.

"Please, Adam, you must not do this!" Renita shrieked.

But he had to. In the space of a few hours he had been pursued, captured, beaten up, and humiliated and it mattered not that Bradley Engles was the instrument responsible for the worst that had happened to him. Engles was the available target to represent to everyone else in San Francisco who Steele had reason to hate. The gray-bearded man, Rod Stockton, the cultured Martha Craig, Angelo who had beaten up on Renita, and the coldly calculated Dwight Newman. He wanted to kill every last one of them. But right now, he had just this one man at his mercy. And he showed none. Did not relax his grip on the scarf and lower Engles's head to the floor until the bounty hunter's mouth had ceased to work and the staring, bulging eyes had taken on the glaze of death.

Then he sighed and had to make a great effort to get up from his knees. When he was erect and had controlled the vertigo of over exertion that threatened to topple him, he draped the scarf back around his neck and looked at Renita.

She was sitting with hunched shoulders on the edge of the bed, holding the Smith and Wesson loosely in her lap as she continued to stare with boundless horror at the bloated, purple-tinged face of the strangled man.

"I owed him."

She looked from the corpse, to the doorway which spilled light into the room, to Steele, and then fixed her stare back on the body of Brad Engles. Her slumped shoulders trembled.

"I am so afraid, Adam," she rasped.

"But still alive," the Virginian drawled as he swept his unemotional gaze over the length of the inert body. "Not like him. He had a real heart-stopping experience."

Chapter Nine

STEELE'S jaw was blackened on both sides by the blows from Engles's fists and both his lips were swollen and scarred by cuts. In the light of the kerosene lamp which stood on a table just outside the door the marks of the beating robbed his features of what slight claim to handsomeness they had ever made.

Standing beside him and shooting frightened glances toward his profile, the woman had to steel herself against the threat of quaking as she saw clearly the latent killer instinct in the man: something that she had never recognized before. And she was certain that in his present tense mood, she would have detected this dark side of his character even if she had not only moments before watched while he strangled the life from a helpless man. Engles's suit jacket, which hung over the back of the chair beside the table, and a smoking cheroot the bounty hunter had left in the crowded ashtray on the table, served to sharpen the images of the recent memory which would not leave her mind.

They stood outside the open door for a full minute, Renita dejectedly and Steele tensely. She was empty-handed and her punished face wore a vacant expression. He gripped the .38 revolver in his gloved right hand and frowned as he listened for sounds from below.

Silence seemed to have a palpable presence in the enormous warehouse: to cause the damp, cold, pre-dawn air to tremble.

The Virginian looked at the woman, pressed a forefinger to his lips, and took a first tentative step toward the faint glow of yellow lamplight that showed at the head of the stairway on the other side of the loft. She followed him, her bare feet making hardly any sound at all. The rustle of the skirt of her dress around her legs was louder.

There was just a square hole in the floor where the stairs ended and he crouched down at the side of this to peer toward the source of the light.

Another kerosene lamp. On the floor, perhaps still in the same position where Martha Craig had set it down just as the beating had started. A few feet away from the door through which they had all entered. Three people slept in unfurled bedrolls on the floor in the brightest pool of light from the lamp. Off to one side, something small glinted and Steele pursed his lips and released a small sigh as he saw his Colt Hartford leaning against the wall, the engraved plate on the stock catching the light.

He eased out of the loft and onto the first tread of the stairway, placing his foot slightly on the plank. He knew the range was too long for the small .38 revolver to be effective, but he kept it aimed at the sleeping form of Dwight Newman who was, as far as he knew, the only one of the trio to be armed—with an identical short-range gun to the Smith and Wesson he held.

Just the rapid, frightened breathing of the woman told him she was close behind him as he climbed down the stairway and moved across the littered floor of the warehouse.

Newman slept in isolation on one side of the lamp. Martha Craig and her grandson had unfurled their bedrolls close to each other on the other side. Strangely, it was the woman who snored softly. Both the men slept almost silently.

As he neared the bedded-down trio, Steele became more conscious of the sound of his footfalls, and ten yards short of his objective he came to a halt. Renita bumped into him and he snapped his head around: silenced her intended gasp with a cold stare of his eyes.

She looked hurt and he spared her a brief smile. Then pointed down at his own feet and hers: moved her head gently with his free hand and gestured with the revolver toward the Colt Hartford leaning against the wall. She shifted her gaze to the rifle, to the blanket-draped form of Newman which blocked a direct route to it, back to Steele. And shook her head, biting at her lower lip.

The Virginian controlled an urge to frown his anger. Simply nodded that he accepted her refusal and dropped onto his haunches to start unlacing his boots. Then Renita touched his shoulder and squatted beside him, reached out a hand to pull his head so that her lips almost brushed his ear as she whispered:

"All right, Adam. I will try for you. But you must promise me something, *mi amor*."

He responded with a quizzical look.

"I was dismayed to see you kill Engles, Adam. But of them all, I liked him the least. The others must not be harmed, though. Newman saved my life at Guerrero. Señora Craig and Angelo have fine reasons for wishing Vettori dead. As I do. You must promise me that you will not hurt them."

He did not hesitate before he nodded agreement to her demand. Then qualified his assent by rasping into her ear: "Unless you or I are threatened, Renita."

She did not nod. Simply straightened up and moved forward, going off at a tangent to encircle all three sleepers rather than take the risk of stepping over Newman.

114

Steele had every intention of keeping his word. At the time he was choking the life out of Engles, it had not mattered which of the group was his victim. The bounty hunter had simply been unlucky enough to be first in line to suffer the Virginian's seemingly insatiable lust for revenge. But now Steele felt he had expunged his hatred for the group as a whole. He wanted only to escape from them and concentrate his efforts on locating the gray-bearded man and force a confession to the murder of Lotus Blossom from him.

His body still pained him, but his mind was clear and cool thinking again. To the extent that he could survey the three sleepers as Renita cautiously circled him, and be pleased he had killed the one—from his own viewpoint—who most deserved to die. Just as she got close enough to the rifle to lean forward and reach out her hands to touch it, Angelo coughed, his body jerking sharply under the blanket.

Perhaps he would not have come awake. And perhaps the other two would have slept on peacefully as well. But ever since he had become enmeshed with this oddly assorted group of fanatics bent on assassination, Steele had always lost out by waiting for others to make the first move. Until he set in motion the plan to escape from the warehouse.

Renita froze, fear fixing a tighter hold on her punished face as she snapped her head round to stare at Angelo.

"Throw it to me!" Steele snarled. And lunged toward Dwight Newman, his gun hand thrust out to the fullest extent of his arm's reach.

The bounty hunter grunted.

Angelo cried: "*Que . . . ?*"

Martha Craig was interrupted in mid-snore and returned to awareness with a choking sound.

"Renita!" the Virginian demanded at the top of his voice, the name resounding between the high walls of the warehouse.

Her enormously enlarged eyes sped their stare from Newman, to Steele, and to the Colt Hartford. Then her hands moved almost as fast. She snatched at the rifle with both hands, drew it back against the front of her body, and hurled it forward.

The stock missed Newman's head by no more than an inch as the bounty hunter folded up into a sitting position: hurling aside his blanket and jerking his gun hand clear. He could have a bullet into the woman's body across a range of less than six feet, but recognized the thudding footfalls of Steele as a sign of the true danger.

"Dwight!" Mrs. Craig shrieked, as she rolled over and raised onto all fours.

Angelo clutched the blanket closer to his body, as if he thought it offered some kind of protection.

Steele came to an abrupt halt and triggered a shot from the .38 revolver. He did not attempt anything fancy for he knew his limitations. When he was a cavalry officer he carried and

116

used a revolver. And during the first few weeks of the violent peace he owned a small two-shot derringer. But he had never liked or trusted handguns and he never acquired more than average skills with them.

So now he fired merely for effect, his bullet ricocheting off the floor in a spray of cement chips. Close enough to Martha Craig to force a scream of terror from her throat.

The gunshot and scream acted to interrupt the smooth movements of Dwight Newman as he turned his torso and swung his gun toward Steele. The Virginian had time to drop the revolver, crouch, and get his gloved hands in just the right attitude to catch the rifle around the frame and barrel. His left thumb cocked the hammer, his right forefinger curled the triger, and he arced the Colt Hartford down to aim at the bounty hunter from the hip.

Newman froze, his gun fractionally off target: his impassive expression a match for that of Steele.

"Another inch and you'll be aiming to get a hole in the head, feller," the Virginian drawled.

"Don't, Dwight!" the old woman advised shrilly.

"Relax, Martha. I've lived as long as I have by knowin' when I'm beaten. Where d'you want the gun, Steele?"

"About where I dropped Engles's."

Newman leaned to press the revolver to the floor, then slid it across toward its mate.

"Where is Brad?" Newman wanted to know.

"He is dead," Renita blurted. "It could not be helped."

The old woman and Angelo looked more afraid than ever. Newman accepted the revelation with equanimity.

"So he finally used up all his luck," he said evenly as Steele stooped and aimed the rifle one-handed for a couple of seconds as he picked up the two revolvers and pushed them into a pocket of his jacket. "He never was much if I wasn't around to take care of him."

"Now he's nothing at all," Steele answered as he took sideways steps to get close to the trembling Angelo.

The young Mexican uttered a choked cry as the aim of the rifle was shifted away from Newman and the muzzle rested gently on the center of his forehead.

"Adam!" Renita gasped.

"Easy," the Virginian told Angelo. "She has sympathy for you people and I can understand that. So I promised her I wouldn't kill any of you unless I had to."

"Brad didn't know when he was beaten, huh?" Newman asked sardonically.

"My knife, feller," Steele instructed Angelo. "And the door key."

"*Si.*"

He continued to gaze coldly down at the Mexican but spoke to Newman. "As Renita told you, it wasn't supposed to have happened. I reckon he knew he was beaten. I just didn't know I'd won until he was dead."

Angelo was stretched out flat on his back. The blanket moved as his hands delved under it. The knife and the key were produced and laid on the floor. The Mexican's hands gripped the top of the blanket again and hauled it up so that he was covered from throat to feet.

The Colt Hartford was held one-handed again, covering nobody in particular, as Steele slid the knife into the boot sheath and called Renita's name before tossing the key toward her. She caught it clumsily and possession of it seemed to deepen her terror.

"Let's go," he explained, with a nod at the door.

"I guess it's no good tellin' you you're safer here with us than out on the streets," Newman said as Renita turned and hurried toward the door while Steele moved more slowly, shuffling backwards.

"He is right!" Martha Craig added, her fear displaced by a brand of pathetic helplessness as she rose painfully to her feet, her elderly body protesting at the exertion.

"You're talking to a feller who's done a lot of gambling," the Virginian told them as he heard the key turn in the lock and then felt a cool, damp draft of ocean air as the door swung open. "Reckon the odds against me finding the killer of the whore are pretty long. But I like them better than the deal you people set up."

"You really didn't kill her?" Newman asked, surprised.

"That's right."

"Well, I never," the bounty hunter responded, shaking his head.

"I know you didn't," the Virginian countered, backed out the door, and kicked it closed. He took the key from the still-frightened woman, turned it in the lock and left it there. "Come on."

He took a step away from her, then had to turn, grip her arm and force her to move. She had become so withdrawn that she vented a strangled cry of alarm at his touch. And she stared at him for stretched seconds in deep horror until her mind cleared.

"Where are we going, Adam?"

"Away from here."

He let go of her and took long strides, covered several yards before he heard the slap of her bare feet on the cement as she ran to catch up with him. The misty night was still clamped firmly on the city, the air coming in off the bay running damp, moist tendrils over their exposed flesh and penetrating their clothes. The breath they expelled turned to white vapor as it left their lips.

Steele set a fast pace, heading south between the rear of the warehouses and the railroad tracks. He carried the Colt Hartford sloped to his shoulder, but with his thumb to the hammer as he strained his ears and raked his eyes constantly from left to right. Three times Renita whispered the first word of a question, but on each occasion a terse shake of his head drove her back into silence.

They were moving through a still world colored gray and black. The gray of mist and the black of buildings. Steele's footfalls on cement masked the muted sound of the woman's tread. Her rapid breathing covered his own.

When he made a sudden left turn to go between a pair of towering warehouses she gasped her alarm and had to run several paces to catch up with him again.

"Adam, where are we going?" she demanded tensely.

"I'm going back to where it started," he answered as they emerged onto the open area of the dockside. "That's the easy part. You're the problem."

"I want to come with you."

They had come to a halt. She stared hard at him while he surveyed the mist-shrouded waterfront. She continued to express fear: he was impassive.

"Be grateful if you'd just do as I tell you, Renita," the Virginian drawled absently, eyeing a vista which was little different to that at the rear of the warehouses because of the mist. Except that now there were buildings on just one side. On the other the prows, sterns, superstructures, and riggings of moored ships loomed darkly against the gray curtain that hung over

San Francisco Bay. "And right now I want you to be quiet and stay close to me. Some or maybe all these ships will have men aboard standing watch. Come on."

He moved forward again, but less hastily and more quietly than before. The woman matched his pace, obviously resenting his attitude toward her. And although he understoood her feelings, he neither said nor did anything to assuage them. For single-minded purpose of locating the gray-bearded man allowed him no time and very little inclination to consider side issues. And right then Renita was precisely that—a side issue who was also an encumbrance. But one he had to endure because he owed her for the freedom he was enjoying. Which pricked his conscience with pangs of guilt as she tracked him along the waterfront like a faithful and trusting puppy dog.

Then she became useful to him again. As he led her toward the entrance of the ferry slips area at the foot of Market Street. The gate was invitingly open, but a uniformed man stepped from a nearby shack just as Steele and the woman were about to move out onto the *Embarcadero*. He was tall and broad and his right hand was fisted around the butt of a revolver in its unfastened holster. His face was just a pale blob below the visor of his cap. His voice was youthful and tough sounding.

"What the hell you people doin' around here this time in the mornin'?" he demanded.

Renita caught her breath noisily and gripped Steele's upper arm with clawed fingers.

"That's kind of a personal question, feller," the Virginian replied, forming his lips into the line of a leer.

If the guard could see the expression he did not respond in the way Steele had hoped.

"Ain't no one but ferry passengers and the people who run the ferry allowed this side of the gate. That's days. At nights, ain't no one allowed."

"But, *señor*," Renita said in a coy tone before the Virginian could voice his own counter to the guard's intractable response, "what we have been doing cannot be done in the day time. Not unless the mist is as thick as it is now."

She sniggered as she released her grip on Steele's arm and sidled forward, accentuating the naturally provocative sway of her hips.

"What's that?" The guard was obviously dull-witted and only now on the brink of realizing what the couple were hinting at.

"We had a little too much wine, *señor*," the woman went on. "And took it into our heads to enjoy each other in a small boat. You understand 'enjoy,' *señor*? But the boat, it was not tied securely. And we were too busy with each other to know this. And we sleep until the boat . . . it hits something and we wake."

"I don't give a damn about that," the guard growled. "You're not supposed to be here and I'm gonna have to . . ."

"Señor," Renita cut in as she halted immediately in front of him, hands on her hips and belly thrust forward. "If we did not sometimes do what is not right, life would be most dull, would it not?" Now she raised her hands to cup each of his cheeks. "If you will promise not to tell anybody of this, you and I can go into your cabin and . . ."

"Get away from me, you dirty little whore!" the guard snarled, bringing up his own hands to wrench hers off his face as he jerked away from her.

But the woman had done what was required of her by then: got the man's hand away from the gun butt and allowed Steele time to swing down the Colt Hartford, cock the hammer, and step to the side to level the rifle at him.

"All right, feller," the Virginian said, causing the man to shift his gaze away from Renita. His expression changed from revulsion to anger. "You're doing a fine job here. But if you keep trying they'll have to find a replacement."

The guard, who was not as young as he sounded, opened his mouth to give voice to his anger. But then he blocked the words as a memory was dredged from the back of his mind. While his attention was directed at Steele, Renita moved to the side, deftly took the Frontier Colt from his holster, and scuttled away from him.

"I heard about you, mister," he growled.

124

"You're the fancy dresser that killed the Chinese whore over at the Havelock Hotel."

"The way you feel about such women, why should you care?" Renita asked, with a strange vehemence in her tone.

"You talk to anyone else about that, you tell them I didn't do it, feller," Steele said.

"What you gonna do to me, mister?" The guard was afraid now, his tongue darting out to lick his lips.

The Virginian saw this clearly: also the swarthy features of the man's face. For the first dull streaks of daybreak were beginning to probe through the darkness of night.

"Is there a lock on the door of your shack?"

He nodded.

"The key?"

"In my coat pocket."

"Give it to the young lady."

"What if I don't?" His bravado lacked force.

"Then maybe I'll kill you."

The guard gulped, pushed a hand into his pocket, and pulled out a bunch of keys. Without being asked, he sorted out the one required and gripped it between a thumb and forefinger to offer the whole bunch to Renita. She took it at arm's length and then followed him at a safe distance as he turned in compliance with a gesture of the Colt Hartford and headed into the shack.

"I could get fired for lettin' this happen to me," he complained from the dark interior.

"Better than me firing this rifle, I reckon," Steele responded, and nodded for the woman to close and lock the door.

She did so, then sighed her relief and sagged against the clapboard wall.

The Virginian showed her a brief, boyish grin. She acknowledged it with a wan smile.

"I did not enjoy making such a pretense, Adam," she murmured, allowing the key to slip from her hand and clatter to the cobbles in front of the shack.

"You did fine," he assured her.

"I can come with you?"

"Don't see how I could make it without you, Renita. Seems you've become my key helper."

Chapter Ten

IT WAS only a short distance from the ferry slips entrance to the Havelock Hotel and Steele and Renita had the *Embarcadero* to themselves as they crossed the broad street in the first light of the misty dawn. The windows of the hotels and office buildings stared blankly down at them, not one of them showing a light.

A narrow alleyway lined on both sides by rancid-smelling trash cans ran between the Havelock and another, smaller hotel, connecting with the one at the rear of the buildings by which Steele had made his escape the previous evening. Rats scampered out from the storehouses of rotted food as the Virginian led the woman purposefully along the alley, stopping once to discard the two Smith and Wesson revolvers and the Frontier Colt in a trash can.

She was not afraid of the foragers: did not cling to Steele's upper arm until he halted outside the rear door of the hotel.

"I think it is insane to return to this place, Adam," she protested in a rasping whisper.

"Where else could I pick up his trail in a city?" the Virginian growled as he stooped to look at the door lock.

It was a secure one, set into the timber, and he straightened up, knowing he would not be able to slide the lock tongue with his knife. So he turned his attention to a nearby window and tried to peer through it, using his free hand as a shade over his eyes. It was dark inside and the window was coated with a thick layer of dust held in place by the grease of cooking.

From every side of Steele and Renita came the sounds of the city rousing itself in preparation to face the new day. Nothing specific or distinctive. Just a subdued humming that beat against the eardrums: noticeable only because the noise was relative to the total silence that had been clamped over San Francisco a few minutes before.

The Virginian experienced a moment of nostalgia for the countless dawns when he had awakened in his true element—surrounded by the magnificent stillness of mountains, plains, or deserts, his horse the only visible living thing within miles of himself.

Then he crashed the stockplate of the Colt

Hartford against the window pane, feeling the clawlike fingers of Renita dig harder into his flesh as broken shards of glass showered to the floor.

"*Madre de Dios!*" the woman rasped.

Then was again driven into tight-lipped silence by an ice-cold look of Steele's dark eyes. She held her breath involuntarily, and matched the Virginian's tense expression as they both listened for a response to the sudden shattering of glass from inside the hotel or any of the buildings which flanked it and backed on to the other side of the alley.

To Renita the breaking of the window had seemed to be an act of desperation. But Steele considered it just one more calculated risk. All the office buildings in the immediate area of the Havelock would still be deserted at this hour of the morning. While the Havelock itself and the other hotels were host to night people: patrons who did not bed down until they were satiated with the pleasures of the city night, and the suppliers of such pleasures who never rested until the patrons' money stopped flowing. All such people should be soundly asleep as night retreated before the advance of day. But there was a chance this was not so, and this was the calculated risk Steele took.

He waited for a full minute, listening to the distant hum of the city. Then reached in through the jagged-edged hole in the glass to release the catch and open the window. Renita watched him, shaking her head and showing an incredulous look in her eyes.

"It always helps to have right on your side," he told her with another boyish grin.

"We have that, Adam," she replied sadly. Señora Craig and the others, I mean. But we picked the wrong man."

He climbed in through the window and began to breathe air permeated with the stale aromas of old cooking.

"Everyone makes mistakes. You could be making one by staying with me, Renita."

"What else can I do? I have no money and I know nobody in the United States except. . . ." She shrugged and accepted the helping hand he thrust toward her. "Even if that was not so, I would wish to stay with you, *mi amor*."

By accident or design, she pressed her body hard against his as she half fell over the window sill. But the twin pressures of her breasts on his chest and the soft firmness of her thighs, and the base of her-belly aroused no feeling of want in him. Instead, he experienced again a sense of guilt that he could feel nothing more than indebted to her, as he released her hand and moved away to close the window.

Enough gray light entered the room to show its furnishings as black forms and he was able to weave his way across to the door without bumping into anything. Renita stayed close behind him: frightened again but also despondent—as if she had instinctively guessed his precise feelings for her by his lack of response at the window.

Beyond the door was the hotel's restaurant scattered with uncovered, greasy tables encircled by an assortment of chairs. The light of the new day, brightening by the moment, spread across the room from three tall windows which looked out over the *Embarcadero* to the mist-shrouded bay on the other side.

Double, glass-paneled doors stood open and Steele and the woman went between them into the Bay City barroom. The chill, damp atmosphere in here smelled of liquor and tobacco smoke: from the dirty glasses littering the tables and bar and the stepped-on remains of cigars and cigarettes spread over the floor.

The Virginian knew the mixture of smells well, from the mornings when a long card game had finished and he had climbed wearily up the stairs to his room while a sullen-faced Rod Stockton had hurried the other players out of the barroom. The smells had been stronger then, not yet made stale by the passage of time. And the body sweat of heat and tension had been in the mixture. It was obvious that there had been no long game last night.

He started up the stairway, rifle canted to his shoulder and gloved thumb resting on the top of the hammer. The hum of the waking city did not penetrate into the hotel and there were just his own and Renita's footfalls to disturb the silence. Until they reached the balcony and could hear the involuntary sounds of people sleeping.

Eight whores resting bodies wearied by the pretense of passion. The fleshy Madam Mary and her ineffectual husband dreaming of the money made and that which was still to come. The towering Stockton frowning as his subconscious thoughts dwelt on the fruitless pursuit of the Virginian.

From his two weeks' stay at the hotel, Steele knew which door to approach. He halted in front of it and beckoned to Renita to bring her head close to his: then pointed back to the door immediately opposite the top of the stairway.

"Like you to stand over there. If you hear anyone moving about inside the room come and tell me. I'll be in here."

He did not look for a facial response and gave the woman no time to speak, as he turned the handle, pushed open the door, stepped across the threshold, and closed the door behind him. Her bare feet carried her along the balcony, making less sound than the scurrying rats had in the alley.

The bedroom was twice as large as any other in the hotel with two windows that admitted early morning light between undrawn silk drape curtains. The bed covers were also silk. But black while the drapes were gold colored. The bed was a white four poster with lace trimming. The rest of the furniture was white, too, with scrollwork around the edges and gold handles on drawers and closet doors. It stood on a black, deep-pile carpet that muted the sound of Steele's tread as he crossed the room, breathing in air that was redolent with the madam's perfume.

He stopped at the side of the bed where the short, thin, rat-faced, sixty-year-old man slept with his mouth gaping and left cheek twitching. Then stooped to press a gloved hand over the open mouth as he rested the muzzle of the rifle against the silk-contoured crotch of the man sprawled on his back.

"Morning to you, feller," the Virginian greeted evenly as the man jerked awake and blinked his eyes several times before they focused clearly on the figure leaning over him.

"Hush until I tell you," Steele said across the mumbling sounds the man made against the palm of his hand, and stooped lower so that his impassive face was no more than six inches above the frightened features of Madam Mary's husband. "Story is that after whoring her way around the world, the fat lady reckons you're the only real man who ever had her. So if I have to shoot off this rifle, it could hurt her as much as it hurts you. Understand?"

Steele raised his hand a little, to allow the man leeway to nod. When the nod came, he removed his hand completely from the suddenly sweat-sheened face. The head was raised off the silk-covered pillow so that he could look down to where the Colt Hartford's muzzle

rested. Then he glanced hopefully toward the
untidy mass of artificially colored blonde hair
at the back of his wife's head. Finally returned
his fear-filled eyes to the Virginian.

"You gotta be crazy, Steele," he gasped.
"Comin' back here."

Steele altered the position of the rifle
slightly, without applying any more pressure.
Reminding the man of his predicament rather
than causing him pain.

"I said to wait until I tell you, feller." He
tried to recall the man's name. He was sure he
had heard it several times, but no memory
flipped forward. Perhaps because he was that
kind of man, his natural lack of distinction emphasized by living constantly in the shadow of
his overbearingly prepossessive wife. He asked:
"What's your name?"

"Clyde!" He swallowed hard but the constricting fear stayed in his throat. "Clyde Barton. Why?"

"No reason. Like you to wake up Madam
Mary."

"She don't like being woke up. Likes to do it
when she's ready. Else she's in a real bad
mood."

"She worry you more than me right now,
Clyde?"

Steele's voice was low-pitched and even. Barton matched the level, but his tone suffered
from a harsh edge of fear.

"That's right. I'm talkin' crazy. But what

d'you expect, wakin' a man the way you did?"

"I expect him to do what he's told, Clyde. You wake her now. And as soon as she is awake, be sure she knows her man won't be a man any more unless. . . ."

"Okay, okay, I've got the message, Steele." The Virginian nodded.

Barton carefully withdrew a skinny hand from under the silk sheets and pushed it gently into the mass of dyed blonde hair. He slept naked, at least above the waist.

"Mary, sweetheart," he crooned softly, his fingers massaging the fat madam's shoulder. "Wake up, darling. And please don't be angry and start yellin', my love."

The woman vented a sigh, then a grunt: both reflexes causing her fleshy body to tremble and shake the bed.

"Mary, sweetheart?"

She smacked her lips and surfaced from sleep. "What?" she demanded, her voice soft and growling.

"Not so loud, Mary. Turn over and look at . . ." He jerked his hand away from her.

"I ain't been to sleep an hour, seems," the hotel madam snarled, pulling herself up in the bed before she rolled on to her back and turned her head.

The torso she thus exposed was also naked. An enormous area of stark white flesh featured with the jet black hair at her armpits and the large patches of dark brown on the crests of the distorted half orbs of her sagging breasts. Above her bulging shoulders and neck her thick-set features were smeared with color—the reds of lip makeup and rouge, the brown of powder and the black and green of mascara. A night face in ruins. At her best, Madam Mary could look fat and forty. Now she appeared gross and past sixty. Body sweat mixed with the perfume she exuded.

Mere irritability expanded to rage as her blue eyes looked out from between folds of fat to take in the scene before them.

"Don't yell, Mary, or . . ."

"I'll shoot his balls off," Steele cut in evenly on the terrified Barton. "Hear that will deprive the both of you."

"You . . ." the word emerged close to a shriek. The Virginian's thumb clicked back the Colt Hartford hammer and the woman compressed her lips, then opened them again to finish in a whisper: ". . . wouldn't dare!"

"Don't take the chance, sweetheart!" her husband pleaded and made to touch her again. But he snatched his hand away as she hauled up the sheets to cover her gross nudity.

"What do you want, Steele?" She had brought her anger under control. But there was no fear to replace it. Instead her small eyes registered an expression of arrogant distaste. "To ask me to call off the reward? No chance. Lotus Blossom was bringin' a lot of money into this place. And you ain't gonna get away with killin'

136

her. Which you would do if I left it up to the local law to hunt you. They'll likely pin a medal on a man instead of hangin' him for killin' a whore!"

"You finished?" Steele asked.

"No I friggin' ain't! I want that five grand you took off Lotus Blossom. That's what's gonna pay the reward. So you better still have it when you're caught, mister. Or I'll cut pieces outta you one at a time and sell them to the quack doctors that buy them kinda things."

"Please, sweetheart," the quivering, sweat-run man at her side implored. "Listen to him and then maybe he'll go."

"Don't worry, husband," she replied. "He harms one hair on your balls, you yell and Stockton'll come runnin'."

"Madam Mary," Steele said softly.

"Yeah?"

"Shut your damn mouth. Or I'll kill you and mark down the Chinese whore as just a bad experience."

A volatile temper had once been one of the Virginian's major character faults, but he had learned to control it: to turn hot rage into ice-cold anger which aided calm thought rather than hindered it. But on occasions he could come dangerously close to reacting prematurely, leaving himself open to the threat of a reckless response to the moves or even words of another.

Now was such an occasion, as he found himself in a dominant position and yet on the defensive against the fat whorehouse madam. His resentment at this paradox found outlet in a hatred toward her that was so deep he could taste it. He meant what he said and this sounded in the rasping tone of his voice and showed in the intensity of the stare he directed at her.

Her husband heard and saw the depth of Steele's feeling first, took a sharp intake of breath and held it. Perhaps a full second later the woman realized she had talked her way to within a hairsbreadth of violent death.

She seemed about to voice a question, but in the tense silence that followed the Virginian's threat no line of his expression had softened. And she licked both smeared lips before pressing them tightly together.

Steele pursed his own lips, nodded, and murmured: "Grateful to you. Awhile back you asked me why I came here. Well, I didn't kill your girl and this is the first I've heard about any money being stolen. Five thousand is a lot of cash for a whore to have in a place like this, isn't it?"

The heat of rage had died down now and his face had returned to its normal impassive set. Madam Mary stoked her own anger, but her husband sensed this and warned:

"Stay calm, my dear. Don't provoke him again."

The woman teetered on the edge of vehemence, then sighed. "All right, Clyde. For you, lover. I told you, Steele, that Lotus Blossom made a lot of money for us. She was the best liked girl here. And the one with most sense. She didn't fritter away what she made for herself on foolish trifles. She saved it. Had ambition, did poor Lotus Blossom. To run a house of her own. In New Orleans."

Madam Mary spoke very softly, in a tone of genuine regret, her normally avaricious eyes troubled by sad recollections. But abruptly she snapped herself out of this melancholy mood and seemed momentarily ashamed of showing a side of her character not normally seen.

"She'd saved that money over three years here. Kept it hid in a tin box under a loose floorboard in her room. Only me and her knew where it was. Until you . . ."

"Forget about me," Steele interrupted. "Tell me about the feller with the gray beard?"

"What?"

"I know *what* he is. He's a killer. Like to find out who he is. Better still, where he is."

The Virginian knew his question had struck a vein of knowledge in the minds of both Madam Mary and Clyde. For the surprise the couple expressed came close to incredulous shock.

"You mean . . ."

"Shut up, Clyde!" Madam Mary snapped. "What kinda shit you tryin' to stir to cover yourself, Steele?"

"I've been dropped into that up to my neck,

lady. And the only way I can get out is to find the tall, thin feller with a gray beard who shot the whore."

"That's crazy. He wouldn't . . ."

"Who wouldn't?" Steele cut in, the demand rasping through clenched teeth.

"Roscoe Karpis," Clyde supplied grimly.

"I told you to . . ."

"Shut your own mouth, Mary!" the skinny man told his obese wife, his sudden firmness shocking her into silence. "I ain't gonna risk gettin' gelded on account of you havin' a soft spot for that no-good sonofabitch."

The madam's complexion under the smeared cosmetics was abruptly an angry shade of purple. Her lower lip dropped and her flesh-crowded eyes blazed as she prepared to snarl at Clyde. But what emerged from her gaping mouth was a strangled gasp—as Steele shifted the muzzle of the Colt Hartford from the man's crotch to the center of her bulbous belly.

"Best that for once you do as he says, lady," the Virginian growled. "Wouldn't you say? No, best you say nothing."

"Damn you, Clyde," she whispered, then compressed her lips and tried to scare him into silence with a menacing glare.

But he refused to look at her, and began to talk fast to Steele. "Karpis was the girl's beau, mister. Never has been around much on account of he's a seaman on the clipper ships. But the girl hardly ever stopped yakkin' about him when he was away. And would've been with him every spare minute she had while he was here—if he hadn't been on the town drinkin' and gamblin' and whorin'. Trouble was, he only ever came around to get money off her when his own roll ran out."

"She loved him," the madam said, her rage subsided now that she realized the battle of wills with her husband had been lost. "There aren't many girls in this trade who are able to feel that for a man. He was gonna be her partner in the New Orleans house."

"He was takin' her for a friggin' ride," Clyde countered. "You was always so blinded by that romantic shit you never could see that, Mary. Same as she was."

"Anyone see this feller go up to her room last night?" Steele asked.

"He was in early, doin' some drinkin'," Clyde answered. "I had to go out and he was gone when I got back. Fifteen minutes or so before the killin'. Maybe he come up here with her. I .dunno. You see anythin', Mary?"

The woman pressed her lips so close together they seemed to disappear.

Clyde shrugged. "I guess maybe one of the bartenders or croupiers could help you, mister. And Rod Stockton."

"Not if they want to keep their friggin' jobs," Madam Mary rasped. "No one workin' for me is gonna help this punk frame Roscoe."

"But he could be tellin' the truth," Clyde said

thoughtfully. "You said only you and Lotus Blossom knew about the money under the floorboards. But Karpis must have known about it too."

"Sure he did," the woman allowed. "And I ain't denyin' the girl wouldn't have had a lot more saved if he didn't come around for handouts." She glared accusingly at Steele. "But ain't there some sayin' about not killin' the goose that lays the golden eggs? And Roscoe didn't play poker for near two weeks, tryin' to win a bankroll and endin' up flat broke."

The Virginian had got more than he had expected from his return visit to the Havelock Hotel. He had just one final question for the eagerly cooperative Clyde Barton: "Where's Karpis now, feller?"

"Right now is anybody's guess, mister. But I know he's shippin' out for the Orient on the *Lady Jane* later today."

Steele nodded and withdrew the threat of the rifle from Madam Mary. "Grateful to you."

He felt drained and weary and there were good reasons for this. During his stay as a guest at the hotel the normal routines of days and nights had been reversed. So, as the rising sun began to burn off the damp mist from the city and bay, his body clock signaled the time for sleep. And the demand was more insistent than usual because of the beating he had taken at the Filbert Street warehouse. Compounding his weariness was the prospect of what he still had

142

to do. Locate the gray-bearded Roscoe Karpis and find proof that the seaman had killed the whore. In a city peopled with countless money-hungry men who were ready to shoot him on sight, and who would remain so inclined until it was accepted without doubt that Karpis was the killer.

"You ain't friggin' welcome," Madam Mary snarled.

Her husband once more displayed cool practical sense in face of her crass irascibility. "What d'you plan for us, mister?"

Steele's abruptly weary brain had not thought that far ahead. And when Clyde's dully spoken query forced him to confront the problem, he realized he had to deal with many others. Getting out of the Havelock Hotel without giving the couple in bed an opportunity to raise the alarm was only the initial step toward the aim he had been considering in theoretical outline. He then had to move along city streets which would already be filling with pedestrian and vehicular traffic. Get back on the waterfront, locate the berth at which the *Lady Jane* was moored, isolate Karpis, and prove murder in the presence of reliable witnesses.

Once again he indulged in a moment of wishful thinking. That he was not trapped within the confines of a city, but was out in open country where the solution to his quandary would be simple: where, given that he abided by his own moral code, a man could do what he felt he had to do and still be able to sleep nights. Perhaps that was also possible in a place like San Francisco, but the Virginian was not experienced enough to be sure of this: felt strongly influenced by the metropolitan environment and society.

"I'm sorry, Adam," Renita groaned, close to tears.

The door had opened and he whirled toward the sound, swinging the Colt Hartford from his hip. The Mexican woman stood rigidly on the threshold, her head bent awkwardly to one side under the pressure of the muzzle of a Remington revolver that was held against her neck. Her long black hair had been pulled back to reveal the whole length of the gun barrel. The butt of the revolver was gripped in the right fist of Dwight Newman. The hammer was cocked to add emphasis to the threat emanating from the ice-cold eyes of the bounty hunter.

"You come with us or she goes to meet her maker, Steele," Newman rasped.

"What the hell's goin' on?" Madam Mary demanded.

The Virginian could have put a killing bullet into the bounty hunter and taken his chances of reaching the open street: perhaps finding it necessary to kill Martha Craig, Angelo, or Rod Stockton if any or all of them tried to stop him. For he felt sufficiently impatient and frustrated to plunge into such a desperate escape bid. But such a reckless act would certainly cost Renita

144

her life and this was a price he knew he was not prepared to pay. Even though he could look at the pathetically pleading expression on her bruised and cut face and ignore it. It was a decision based entirely on what was behind his own battered face, deeply imbedded in his mind, that caused him to let the Colt Hartford barrel sag toward the carpet.

"Shut up, Mary," Clyde advised. "I don't figure this is any of our business."

"It friggin' well is! Hey mister, I've posted a five thousand-dollar reward for this little runt. You take that rifle off him and leave him here, the money's yours."

Her excitement quivered in the words as she spat them from her smeared lips.

"Lady, you're talking the business I used to be in," Newman replied wryly. "But right now I've got other things on my mind. Come on outside, Steele. And let Angelo take that rifle and knife off you."

His free hand was hooked over Renita's shoulder. When he tugged at her, she was forced to back out of the doorway at the same pace as he did.

"Stockton!" Madam Mary shrieked, high-pitched with the rage of desperation, as Steele advanced on the doorway.

Angelo and Martha Craig stepped into view on the balcony to either side of Newman and Renita.

"Be silent, you over-painted old harridan,"

Mrs. Craig snapped, her emaciated face host to a sneer of revulsion as she peered into the bedroom. "It will take more than a loud noise to wake up that big ox of a man."

"You've killed him!"

"Merely ensured he remains asleep, woman!" came the sneering retort. "If you wish to receive the same treatment, you have only to open your slut's mouth again!"

Like Newman, Angelo was not wearing his suit jacket. Both had gun belts slung around their waists. As the old woman spoke, the young Mexican drew a Colt .45 from his holster, held it by the barrel, and thudded the butt against his palm.

"The creatures who sell their bodies in this evil establishment have been given a similar offer," Mrs. Craig went on in the same tone. As if each word was a globule of foul-tasting saliva she was spitting out.

As Steele stepped from the bedroom onto the balcony, Angelo gripped the butt of his Colt and leveled the revolver at the Virginian until the transfer of rifle and knife had been completed.

"You really are a hard man to convince, aren't you, Adam Steele," Martha Craig murmured as Clyde Barton whispered placating words to his incensed wife. "We really do intend for you to carry out your part of our plan, you know."

"I am sorry, *mi amor*," Renita forced out miserably.

"You must not be sorry, my dear," the old woman assured, turning to lead the way along the balcony toward the head of the stairs. "Your treachery toward us has turned out for the best, has it not? By winning the heart of Adam Steele you have dealt us the winning card."

"And you look like you're a bad loser," Newman growled, nodding to indicate that Steele should move in the wake of Mrs. Craig.

"One thing's for sure," the Virginian drawled. "At losing you people, I'm no good at all."

Chapter Eleven

THE DOORS to the whores' rooms remained firmly closed. A glance through the only other open door on the balcony showed Steele the blanket-contoured form and exposed back of the head of Rod Stockton. There was a dark stain on the pillow beneath the unmoving head.

At the rear of the slow-moving procession, Angelo said into the plushest room of the house: "If either of you comes out before we leave, I will shoot them."

Down in the barroom, the group had to halt while Martha Craig shot the bolts and opened the double doors that gave onto the *Embarcadero*. When she opened them, warm air smelling strongly of the ocean flowed into the hotel. Everyone blinked against the dazzling reflection of sunlight on water. Every trace of the night mist had gone from the atmosphere and the heat haze of day had not yet started to shimmer. Between gaps in the waterfront shacks on the other side of the street, the buildings of Oakland and Alameda showed up starkly in black and white against the green hills behind the towns.

The lettering adorning the side of the enclosed wagon parked immediately outside the Havelock Hotel entrance was black on yellow: CRAIG CONSTRUCTION COMPANY—SAN FRANCISCO. EST. 1849.

"Ain't exactly what you'd call luxury," Newman said, using his own and the woman's body to shield the gun while they crossed the sidewalk to the rear of the wagon. "But I guess it beats hoofin' it away from here with a trigger-happy mob on your trail."

Martha Craig opened the doors at the back of the wagon while Angelo closed those of the hotel. Steele climbed aboard first, then Renita. Newman and Angelo got into the wagon together. Then the old woman closed the doors from the outside, blocking off the sunlit view of a street busy with early-morning activity. Riders and wagons were moving on the street and people were about on the sidewalks making distinctive and separate sounds against a background of the city's hum. Hooves clacked and wheel rims rattled on the street paving. Men shouted. Doors and window shutters were banged open. The water of the bay slurped against the dockside and piers.

Everyone was in a hurry, intent upon the business they had in hand: and had no reason to pay any attention to the people who emerged from the hotel and climbed on the wagon. Or to the wagon itself a few moments later as it rolled from a standstill at a sedate pace, with Martha Craig up on the seat in control of the two-horse team.

The atmosphere in the enclosed body shell was humidly warm and smelled of cement. The sunlight that penetrated through the cracks around and between the two rear doors was easy on the eyes. Dwight Newman and Angelo stood upright, leaning against the doors, their guns holstered but their eyes fixed on Steele and Renita, who sat on the dusty floor at the front of the wagon: the woman once more drawing comfort from gripping the Virginian's upper arm.

Fear seemed to glisten in the low light from every sweat bead on her forehead and jaw. Steele's feelings were accurately displayed on his bristled face, which expressed calm resignation. Which had been established from the moment Martha Craig opened the hotel doors and he saw the construction company wagon: when any inclination to attempt an immediate escape was swept away. For the wagon was a perfect way for him to move along the dangerous streets of the city. And its destination was the abandoned warehouse. In the same waterfront area where a clipper named *Lady Jane* was moored.

"You shouldn't have told us you were goin' to look for the guy who shot the whore, Steele," Newman said, less tense-faced now the wagon had rattled away from the Havelock Hotel without hindrance from those left behind. "We figured there was only one place you could start lookin'."

"I did not see them, Adam," Renita muttered miserably. "I was looking all the time at the door you told me to. When I hear them they are on the stairs. With their guns pointing at me. I should not have been afraid for my life."

"Sure you should," he assured her evenly.

"You made it easy for us," the bounty hunter went on. "Breakin' the window the way you did. And leavin' her right where we could see her and get the drop on you."

"But you're in no mood to return favors, I reckon?"

"Damn right!" Newman's expression matched his tone: showing the same degree of hardness he had exhibited when Steele had whirled to see the man on the threshold of Madam Mary's bedroom. "And in no position to pay you back for anything' else, dude! Like killin' my partner!"

"*Señor!*" Angelo said, his voice rasping with

anxiety as he heard the venom in the bounty hunter's voice.

Newman took a few moments to bring his emotions under control, then shrugged and picked up the Colt Hartford from where it leaned in the angle of the wagon's rear and side. He held it in one hand and ran the fingers of the other up and down the polished, fire-scarred stock.

"Relax, kid. I ain't forgettin' the way Vettori cheated me and Brad outta our bounty money and tried to have us gunned down. Even if things weren't the way they are, he'd still be top of my hate list."

Angelo looked from the hard-eyed bounty hunter to the unresponsive face of the Virginian. "Do not be concerned, *señor*," he assured. "Our plans have not been changed because of the death of Engles. You will still be allowed to leave in the way arranged after you kill Hernando Vettori. Señor Newman has given us his word that what is between you and him will be . . ."

"Saved for later, Steele. I move around all over and I figure you do, too. Some time, some place, we'll meet up again. I owe it to Brad."

The Virginian nodded. "Know how you feel, feller. As I recall, you had hold of me while he was throwing the punches."

Newman responded with a nod of his own, as a rueful look spread over his moustached face.

"Yeah, that was pretty stupid of us, wasn't it? Beatin' you up the way we did. We was all agreed on that afterwards."

"Except Engles," the Virginian drawled. "He seemed to get a lot of pleasure out of it."

"But you didn't have to kill him for it!"

"It was my pleasure."

They finished the ride in silence, Martha Craig not having to rein in the team until the way was barred by the gates of the Filbert Street entrance to the dock. When the wagon had rolled through, it was halted again, while she went back to reclose and relock the gates. Then moved forward to slide open one of the large doors at the rear of the warehouse. She did not return to the driving seat: instead led the horses by a bridle. The wagon bumped and rocked crossing the rusted railroad tracks and came to rest finally inside the condemned warehouse. She unfastened the vehicle's doors before she went to slide the building door closed.

"Home sweet home, folks," Newman announced brightly as he and Angelo jumped out of the wagon and gestured with the Colt Hartford for Steele and Renita to follow them.

Daylight entered the building from two sources: down the stairway and through another square hole in the ceiling twenty feet back from the front doors of the warehouse. Immediately below this hole was a pile of hay-bales, stacked two bales high over an area fifteen feet square. Sufficient cushioning for a man to drop the twenty-five feet from the aperture and land without injuring himself.

"Up the stairs, dude," Newman instructed. "And remember little Renita'll pay for the mistake you make if you try to pull anythin' tricky."

Martha Craig and Angelo led the way, Steele was next and the bounty hunter brought up the rear, the cocked Colt Hartford prodding Renita in the back.

"And I don't know what you found out at the whorehouse, but I can still kill you and be a hero if I have to."

"Oh, do be quiet, Dwight," Mrs. Craig chided wearily. "Adam Steele is not a fool and is perfectly aware of the predicament in which he finds himself."

Below there had been no signs that three of the group had spent the night in the derelict warehouse. Up in the loft, preparations had been made for the wait until the ship bringing Hernando Vettori to San Francisco arrived. Against the front wall, to one side of a six-by-six-foot hatch overlooking the dock and piers, were stacked five bedrolls with a cardboard carton on top of them. While Newman kept Renita covered, the woman looked anxiously at Steele, and the Virginian surveyed the vista from the hatch, Martha Craig and Angelo unfurled the bedrolls on the floor and took water canteens and cans and packages of food from the carton.

The sun was now well advanced on its ascent up the eastern dome of the cloudless sky and a shimmering, slick-looking heat haze had drawn a curtain across the landscape on the far side of the bay. The area of bright blue water that could be seen was cut by more than a score of craft which left quickly healed scars of white water in their wakes. A clipper under her full sails, two steamers, a number of ferries, three whalers, and several smaller fishing boats. In the foreground he could see only the ends of the Filbert Street pier and those on either side of it. No craft was berthed against these.

"Stay back from there!" Newman snarled as the Virginian made to move closer to the hatch. "You'll get to see it all when the time comes. Sit your ass down. You as well, Renita."

Angelo indicated the bedrolls on which the prisoners should sit, side by side against the front wall where they could both be watched at once and had no chance to show themselves at the hatch. Their three captors sat opposite them, six feet away, with the supplies in front of Martha Craig. Further back into the loft were the rusted iron brackets where a crane of some sort had been placed. Beyond these was the square hole in the floor. Over in the far corner the chair and table used by the ill-fated Bradley Engles were gone. The door to the windowless office where he died was closed.

"Don't worry," Newman said tensely when he saw Renita gazing anxiously toward the office. "I didn't leave Brad in there. Right now he's feeding the fish with a couple of rocks tied around his waist."

The Mexican woman shivered and pressed her shoulder hard against Steele's.

Martha Craig opened cans and packages. "Breakfast is the only meal we'll have before the monster arrives," she said absently. "Cold, I am afraid. With water instead of coffee."

"I do not want anything," Renita muttered.

"Suit yourself. Adam Steele?"

"Grateful to you."

She pushed a canteen across the floor to him. Then a can of beans and two unwrapped packages containing some jerked beef and a hunk of sourdough bread.

"No eating utensils, but then I am sure you will be able to manage without such luxuries."

The Virginian took off his gloves to eat and discovered the food and water did something to take the edge off his weariness. Newman ate as heartily as he did, while Angelo and Martha Craig did little more than pick at the food.

"You find out anythin' at the whorehouse?" the bounty hunter asked.

"You care, feller?"

A shrug. "We got a few hours to kill. Just fillin' the time."

"I got what I wanted."

"If we do that, all of us will be happy," the old woman said.

They finished the meal in silence, as the noise level from out on the waterfront rose. No sounds came from immediately below the hatch, where the dockside was deserted. But there was a hive of activity to the south as the holds of berthed ships were filled or emptied.

"Why do you wear those old things?" Renita asked as Steele finished rinsing his hands after eating with his fingers, and pulled on the buckskin gloves.

"Habit."

"I thought killers like you wore gloves to keep the blood of your victims off their hands," Mrs. Craig murmured, and shuddered.

"A lot of guys in my trade wear 'em," Newman added.

"Took to wearing them in the war," the Virginian said to the woman sitting at his side as he pressed the buckskin tight between his fingers. "Never can recall quite where or when or why. Nowadays I think of them as a kind of lucky charm. Put them on whenever I reckon there's going to be trouble."

"I've hardly ever seen you with them off, Adam."

"It has got to be that way lately," he drawled.

Silence settled over the group again and Steele leaned his back against the wall and moved his head to tip the brim of his hat down over his forehead, hiding half his face from those who watched him. He felt the side of Renita's face against his shoulder as she, too, experienced the wearying effects of a troubled night without sleep.

As the sun rose higher and grew hotter, it beat harshly on the warehouse roof and penetrated its mounting heat through softened pitch and ancient timber to raise the temperature in the loft. The slight breezes which occasionally danced in off the busy bay and moved through the hatch did nothing to ease the sweating discomfort of the people who sat and waited.

For a while as he rested in the heated silence, Steele suffered the additional unpleasantness of dull aches from the areas where Engles had kneed and punched him. But then the need for sleep became predominant and he listened to the sounds from the waterfront until they became soporific and he allowed himself to drift just below the level of awareness.

It seemed only fleeting moments had passed when he was roused by something banging against one of his booted feet. But as he snapped open his eyes and saw the barrel of the Colt Hartford being withdrawn, he realized he had been asleep for several hours. He knew this from the way he felt—fully rested—and from the way that shadows fell in different directions now and were much shorter in the light from the northeast-facing hatch.

He used both hands to set the Stetson firmly

on his head, then surveyed his surroundings as he felt the sweat beads coursing down his face and heard a new sound from outside.

Renita was no longer at his side. Instead, she sat like a beautiful carved statue on Newman's bedroll.

Newman stood behind her, the Remington in his right hand, its muzzle concealed by the black hair on top of the woman's head.

It was Mrs. Craig who had awakened the Virginian, then backed off, gripping the rifle so tightly that her knuckle joints showed white through the skin of her fingers.

Angelo was gone.

The tension of pent-up excitement showed in every sweat-run line in the faces of the old woman and the bounty hunter. The cones of Renita's breasts rose and fell infinitesimally as her enlarged eyes expressed the depth of her terror.

From immediately below the hatch came a babble of voices, their tone angry.

"It is almost time, Adam Steele," Martha Craig announced, almost reverentially. "The Mexican frigate is about to dock at the pier."

The Virginia felt a stab of self-anger that he had given in to his need for sleep. No. That he had slept for so long. But he did not indulge the emotion, which was futile. The past was dead. As dead as a Chinese whore named Lotus Blossom. It was futile to dwell on what was gone and could never be recovered. Especially when time was dangerously short.

"I can take a look?"

He started to get to his feet before the old woman said: "Very carefully, Adam Steele. Dwight has told you often enough of what will happen if . . ."

She allowed the warning to hang unfinished in the bright, almost unbearably hot air of the loft: satisfied with the way in which the Virginian pressed his back to the wall and screwed his head around the side of the hatch to peer cautiously outside.

The scene out on the bay was much as it had appeared when Steele first looked at it in the morning, with sea sparkling, a variety of craft criss-crossing, and the heat haze shimmering. But closer to his vantage point much had altered.

A frigate, freshly painted and with her metalwork gleaming, was sliding serenely through calm water to dock at the pier that jutted out directly opposite where he watched. Uniformed seamen of the Mexican navy worked with skilled precision to reduce sail as the ship neared her berth. The green, white, and red national flags of Mexico hung limply at the heads of her three masts.

The pier was no longer deserted. A U.S. navy seaman stood ready at each of two bollards where the frigate would be moored fore and aft. Two more were beside a gangway which would be run out as soon as the ship was secured at her berth. Nearby was a group of a half-dozen civilians dressed in frock coats and high hats. From where the group stood a length of red carpet ran shoreward, to finish at the side of the first of a line of three parked landaulettes with liveried drivers up on the seats. The rigs had been cleaned and polished as effectively as the Mexican frigate.

On the warehouse side of the waiting carriages was a scene in marked contrast to the smooth serenity and well-ordered dignity of the official welcome for Hernando Vettori.

About a hundred people, most of them men and all of them Mexican, were grouped together immediately in front of the warehouse—confined there by a half circle of San Francisco police constables with drawn and leveled revolvers. The forty or so lawmen were grim-faced and rock-steady in their stance. And tight-lipped in menacing silence.

It was the Mexicans who muttered angrily to each other and occasionally snarled an insult at the uniformed men who contained them. Some of them carried crudely lettered placards which they held high above the heads of the crowd. The signs, nailed to timber poles, turned as the crowd's frustration and anger found outlet in jostling movement as well as resentful words. The lettering was vivid red on stark white and Steele glimpsed the odd word here and there.

162

Murderer . . . Butcher . . . Treachery . . . Monstruo . . . Asesino . . . Vettori . . . Vettori . . .
Among the placards were several Mexican flags, fluttering in the slipstream as the people who held them rocked the poles to left and right. These showed more scarlet than the flags flying from the masts of the frigate, for they were streaked with paint or perhaps even real blood.

"At first we were troubled that the anti-Vettori demonstration was planned," Martha Craig said as the Virginian shifted his impassive gaze away from the scene immediately below the warehouse to survey the length of waterfront to the right.

"It meant too much law for me and Brad to get in close enough for a shot," Newman growled sourly.

The old woman made an irritable clucking sound at the interruption. Then allowed: "Quite so. But then we realized it was for the best. It would have been difficult for Dwight or Bradley to have escaped unseen after the execution. So we had to commit ourselves to hiring an expert rifle marksman like you, Adam Steele. And in this event, the demonstration will assist all of us."

Beyond the vicinity of the waterfront area scheduled for redevelopment, the port of San Francisco was frenetically busy with its normal daily routine as men and machines worked at loading and unloading the line of ships tied at the piers. Too many ships, too close together in perspective and with many of them partially hidden behind shacks and stacks of cargo for Steele to be able to read any names painted on bows and sterns.

But then, as he shortened the focus of his eyes and dragged his attention back toward the area of the Filbert Street pier, he did a double-take and experienced an uncharacteristic surge of excitment that gave expression to his eyes and caused fresh sweat to ooze from every pore in his body.

"Angelo is down among the crowd," Martha Craig went on and although her words registered in Steele's consciousness, it seemed that he was hearing her voice over an enormous distance. "At precisely the moment when Vettori shakes hands with the state governor, my grandson will fire his pistol into the air. This will undoubtedly cause minor chaos and amid the confusion you will kill Hernando Vettori. There should then be nothing short of pandemonium, which will cover the escape of both Angelo and yourself." There was a pause, then two thuds: one louder than the other. "Here."

The Virginian glanced down at his feet: saw his rifle and a stack of bills, the money held together by an elastic band. He ignored them while he took another look outside at the tall, slim gray-bearded Roscoe Karpis.

The killer of Lotus Blossom was one of a group of about twenty men who stood on the pier next to that where the Mexican frigate was

164

docking. Their clothes marked them as a mixture of longshoremen and seamen. Some were smoking and a few were drinking coffee from battered mugs. Karpis was one of a half-dozen who had seabags slung over their shoulders. In contrast with both the official welcoming party for Vettori and the hate-filled demonstrators, this group expressed either boredom or mild curiosity. They were waterfront workers held up between jobs and seamen killing time until their ships were ready to leave port. Drawn to watch the arrival of the Mexican frigate because they happened to be close by the center of activity and there was nothing else to do.

"Come on, Steele, for Chrissake!" Newman snarled. "Shape up!"

Even Martha Craig's composure began to be strained as she watched Steele stoop and pick up the Colt Hartford. It sounded in her voice and showed in the set of her thin features.

"As soon as you have killed him, you will make your escape in the way that has been explained to you. Dwight, Renita, and I will remain here. Since my company has the contract to pull down this building and Dwight and Renita are temporarily on my payroll, we have every right to be here."

"Don't forget your money, Steele," Newman rasped. And, as the Virginian went down again, picked up the bundle of bills and thrust them into a pocket of his jacket, the bounty hunter hardened his tone. "Somethin' else you should know, in case you figure to take more than money off us."

Steele had owned his father's rifle for so long and used it so often that it was almost an extension of himself. "Reckon I already know it, feller," he said, holding the Colt Hartford in both open palms. "Feels a few shells short."

Newman grinned. "There speaks the expert we know you are, dude. You got just one shot. Make it a good one."

"Vettori's life for Renita's, Adam Steele," Martha Craig said.

"And your own, dude," the bounty hunter added. "You miss, we got no more use for you. And I'll be a hero two times over. Be known as the guy who blasted the killer of the whore: and the couple who planned to murder Hernando Vettori."

"There is only one way, *mi amor*," Renita implored hoarsely. "And it is just that he should die after what he did at Guerrero."

"Don't deny that," Steele murmured as he turned to look out through the hatch again, blinking against the strong sunlight. "What bothers me is that he's just one deserving cause."

Chapter Twelve

THE FRIGATE glided a final few feet through the smooth water under her own momentum, then came to rest against the pier with a creak of straining rope as the two mooring lines were tossed over the side, caught by the U.S. navy seamen and lashed around the fore and aft bollards. A section of rail had already been removed and the gangway was slid smartly into place.

All four uniformed men came to rigid attention as soon as their chores were completed.

The welcoming committee shuffled forward, thrusting sweat-damp handkerchiefs into their pockets and spreading diplomatic smiles across their faces.

Four men in civilian clothes, more suited to the heat of the city, moved across the ship's deck and started down the gangway. One of them was two paces ahead of the others.

The demonstrators began to chant in Spanish, the mass sound waves from their throats seeming to beat against eardrums with a physical force. The red-daubed flags and crudely lettered placards waved to and fro.

The arc of policemen thrust their guns further forward and raked their hard eyes back and forth over the shrieking faces of the Mexicans.

The horses in the traces of the line of carriages snorted and moved uneasily at the abrupt explosion of noise and the liveried drivers cursed as they brought the animals under control—shooting anxious glances toward the angry throng.

An aura of hatred and fear rose up to assault Steele's nostrils: or so he thought until he identified the smell as his own body sweat.

He was standing with his back pressed to the wall, the rifle held two-handed across the front of his thighs, his head screwed around so that his eyes could take in the scene below. In such a position, only half his bristled and bruised face would be seen if anyone should chance to look up at the hatch.

But nobody did.

Those directly concerned with greeting Vettori, protecting him, or hurling invective at him had no inclination for idle glances in other directions. While the group of men on the next pier concentrated their attention on the chanting demonstrators, their interest heightening in expectation of an outbreak of violence.

Steele heard footfalls in the loft, advancing toward him. The lightness of the tread indicated it was Martha Craig who was moving.

He looked briefly at the gangway connecting ship to pier as the short, rotund, broadly smiling Hernando Vettori stepped onto dry land and thrust out his white-gloved right hand.

"Don't crowd me, lady," Steele rasped.

The old woman caught her breath and came to a halt.

The Virginian swung his gaze from one pier to the next.

The Mexican visitor and his American greeter clasped hands.

The volume of shrieked hatred rose to a crescendo.

Steele blinked droplets of sweat off his eyelids.

Angelo Craig fired his Frontier Colt.

Heads snapped around and the chant of hatred was abruptly curtailed. A stretched second of silence in front of the warehouse was invaded from a distance by the normal dockside noises.

A man shouted an order and the half circle of policemen closed in. Fear had replaced hatred in the tone of the massed voices as the Mexican demonstrators pressed into a more close-knit group in face of the menacing advance.

Steele jerked the rifle stock to his shoulder, pressed his cheek against the rosewood and swung away from the wall. The barrel of the Colt Hartford raked over the melee of movement. He became rock still for a split second.

Squeezed the trigger.

Against the higher volume of shrieking voices the report of the rifle shot made no more impression than had the crack of Angelo's revolver.

Steele paused for just one more part of a second: to see the stain begin to spread over the off-white pants leg of Roscoe Karpis. As the seaman started to scream and fall to the pier, the men around him scattering in fear of further shots. Then the Virginian whirled.

Behind and below him, the no longer smiling visitors and their welcoming committee were hurrying along the Filbert Street pier toward the waiting carriages. The senior policeman was yelling orders, designating some of his men to go after the sharpshooter and ordering the rest to herd the Mexican demonstrators into a tighter pack. As countless pairs of anxious eyes flicked their stares in every direction, nobody sure where the second shot had come from.

In front of the Virginian, Martha Craig leaned to the side: her eyes ablaze with excitement as she tried to peer out into the brightly sunlit vista to see if the group's plan had succeeded. Behind her, Dwight Newman snarled a curse as he and Renita scrambled to their feet.

The Mexican woman was no longer under threat of the bounty hunter's Remington. For the man with the moustache was trying to draw a bead on Steele around the skinny frame of Mrs. Craig.

The Virginian had expected the old woman to react as she did. Had also guessed Newman would try to kill him: to remove the danger of his implicating the group. He had not predicted the smiling face of Renita: the smile not of relief, but of triumph as she anticipated looking down on the bullet-shattered body of Hernando Vettori.

He lunged away from the wall, the rifle held like a bar across the front of his body. Then thrust out his arms to the extent of their reach.

"He did not . . . !" the old woman started to shriek, a look of venomous hatred contorting her emaciated features.

"*Bastardo!*" Renita screamed.

The frame of the Colt Hartford crashed into Martha Craig's throat, choking off her words and sending her stumbling backwards.

Newman was coming forward in a half crouch. He was not fast enough in powering to the side and the old woman collided with his hip and did a reverse flip over his stooped back.

Still moving fast, the Virginian released his hold on the stock of the rifle and swung it by the barrel. He aimed for the bounty hunter's gun hand, but the man drew back his arm. The

Colt Hartford continued to swing in the same arc and made thudding contact with Newman's throat. It was the hammer which hit first, with such force that it burst a hole through the leathery skin.

As Martha Craig crashed face down on the loft floor, Newman was knocked upright and then sent sprawling onto his back. The Remington flew out of his hand as a spray of blood spurted from his punctured throat.

Steele did not pause in his forward rush, as Renita lunged into movement—diving for the still sliding revolver as she hurled a string of Spanish invectives at him.

Only as he launched into a leap through the hole in the floor did it occur to him that they might have moved the haybales. But they had been too confident of their plan to take the trouble.

He hit the hay, almost stumbled, but fought to stay upright and then jumped down on to the cement floor of the hot, gloomy, stale-smelling warehouse.

As he raced for the rear doors of the warehouse beyond the parked wagon with the team still in the traces, he glanced back and up over his shoulder.

Renita was crouched there, the bounty hunter's Remington fisted in both her hands, its muzzle tracking him.

"Vettori, woman!" Martha Craig shrieked. "He is the one!"

Steele did not look back again.

No bullets cracked toward him.

He wrenched open the big sliding door through which the wagon had entered and ran out into the sunlight. His legs ached more than when he had made his escape from the Havelock Hotel. And he had never felt so breathless in his life. He forced his mind to consider something other than his physical discomfort.

Renita had completely fooled him. Everything she had done to him or said to him had been part of a trick. And now, as he moved at a stumbling run in the deep shade between two high warehouses, he could look back on their relationship and see the obvious pointers he had failed to spot at the time.

The way she flaunted her body at him when he first saw her. How she had known Angelo did not retie the cut rope even though she had been first to leave the room in the Vallejo Street house. The carefully set trap into which she had led him.

It was obvious now that she had known more than she pretended as she skillfully used her sexuality to strengthen the group's hold on him.

The beating had not been the mistake Newman claimed: had enabled the beautiful Mexican woman to show tenderness as she ignored her own mild injuries to tend to Steele. Which provided the ideal circumstances for her to falsely declare her love for him and to consummate it.

The second escape would not have been in the group's plan. And there had been clues to the deception as first Renita and then Newman had adapted to the unexpected. First the woman had tried to knock out Brad Engles to try to preempt Steele's attack on the bounty hunter. Then, as the man was dying, he had pleaded tacitly with her as she desperately implored Steele to show mercy. A few minutes later, down in the warehouse, the newly awakened Newman could have killed Renita as she reached for the Colt Hartford. Instead, he had wasted valuable time in turning to try for a shot at the Virginian.

It all added up now. Steele thought with a surge of self-anger as he emerged onto the waterfront from between the warehouses. And he was suddenly struck by another idea, which roused revulsion to compound his rage.

The woman had claimed she had been with just one man before Steele and had implied an idyllic romatic relationship with him. Yet she had willingly coupled with the Virginian after knowing him just a few hours: and had been wantonly skillful in bringing him to a climax of pleasure. Had assured him: *"I will know when it is time."* Before this, when he was being told about the evil that occurred in the Sierra Madre village, it had been hinted there was a relationship between Dwight Newman—a drifting bounty hunter—and Renita. After the second escape, while she was expertly flaunting her body to occupy the mind of the guard to the entrance to the ferry slips, she had displayed angry bitterness at the man's contemptuous attitude toward whores.

He came to a breathless halt, raised saliva into his mouth and spat it out on to the dock. But it was not as easy as that to rid himself of the disgust he felt at having penetrated the body of a woman he suspected had been a Mexican village prostitute.

Then a gunshot forced his mind back to more urgent considerations. The single report was quickly followed by a volley. He ran out onto this otherwise empty section of waterfront and skidded to a stop to turn and look up. Over the heads of the shrieking Mexicans and confused policemen toward the hatch in the warehouse loft.

Renita and Martha Craig stood in full view, the younger woman gripping the Remington in both hands to try to steady the bucking action of the recoil while the older one screamed words that were lost in the gunfire and barrage of shouts.

Hoofbeats clattered and wheelrims clanged. Drivers yelled and whips cracked. Splinters of polished wood flew off the first of the three carriages as they raced along the dock toward Steele.

Careful to keep the Colt Hartford tight to his side and aimed down at the ground, the Virginian back-tracked out of the path of the swaying landaulettes. And shifted his gaze back up to the hatch. Just as the policemen angled their revolvers in the same direction.

The fusillade of shots spurred the wagon teams to greater speed and silenced the Mexicans' excitement. Some bullets went high, whining through the hot air above the warehouse roof. Others were wide and thudded into the front to explode splinters of wood fragments from either side of the hatch. Enough hit their intended targets to produce blossoming stains on the women's dresses and open up blood-spouting wounds on their faces.

Both of them were still on their feet as the impact of the hail of bullets drove them staggering back out of sight. But Steele had seen enough to know they would be dead before they collapsed to the loft floor.

Dwight Newman would still be alive up there. Angelo Craig, too, wherever he was. But Steele put the whole bunch out of his mind as he turned and walked on to the pier where Roscoe Karpis lay, on his side and clutching at his shattered kneecap, his bearded face contorted by agony.

The Virginian had good reason for not wanting to think about the group which had tried to trap him into assassinating Hernando Vettori. For he had believed from the start the story Angelo had told him of the massacre at Guerrero. The demonstration by the hate-filled Mexicans and the fanatical last-ditch attempt by the two women to kill the ex-*Federale* served to empha-size that Vettori deserved to die.

And if Steele thought about the matter too deeply, he might feel regret. Regret that the group had not approached him openly: in which circumstance he might have agreed to do what they asked. Of course, such thoughts would be purely academic. But even vague con-templative reflection upon the prospect of being a paid killer made him feel uneasy.

"You!" Roscoe Karpis forced out between gritted teeth as the Virginian approached him.

A sweating, anxious young police constable was down on his haunches beside the injured seaman. The other men who had shared Karpis's vantage point had all run off the pier. Were now watching the action from a closer view-point as some policemen dispersed the demon-strators while others forced open the front doors of the warehouse and plunged inside.

"It's Adam Steele!" Karpis rasped. "The guy who shot my girl at the Havelock Hotel."

The policeman already had his gun in his hand. He aimed it at the Virginian's chest as he powered upright. "Drop the rifle, mister!" he ordered.

Steele rested the stockplate on the pier be-fore allowing the barrel out of his grasp. "It's empty," he said.

"You sure match the description of build and clothes," the constable growled.

"It's him, I tell you!"

177

"He's right," Steele agreed.

The red-faced young lawman was perplexed. He shot a glance toward the warehouse but saw he would get no assistance from there for awhile. "You wing this man?" he blurted suddenly.

The Virginian nodded.

"What the hell for?"

"Make sure he didn't get away. Did you a favor. You get to arrest him for murder."

The lawman's perplexity increased. "Whose murder?"

"He's friggin' nuts!" Karpis snarled.

"The Havelock Hotel whore," Steele said evenly. "If you take a look through his pockets or maybe in his seabag, he'll be carrying something close to five thousand dollars."

"So what?" Karpis demanded hoarsely, with an anxious glance toward the bag which had fallen from his shoulder when he was shot.

"Big roll for a seaman to have."

"I had a lucky streak at a place on the Barbary Coast," Karpis croaked, making his plea up at the lawman, who was less edgy now.

"In the bag, I reckon," the Virginian encouraged. "Maybe still even in a box Madam Mary at the Havelock will be able to identify. Some bartenders and other people at the hotel will be able to testify this feller went up to Lotus Blossom's room a short while before she was shot."

The constable continued to keep Steele covered as he moved in a half circle around the

178

suddenly very frightened Karpis to stoop and pick up the seabag with his free hand.

"It's crap he's talkin'! There was a hundred people in that place heard her yell his name just before she died!"

The lawman could not open the bag one-handed, so he went down on to his haunches to work at it.

"Been thinking about that," the Virginian drawled, gazing absently out across the sun sparkling bay. "She sure seemed to call out Adam Steele. But she was Chinese and she was terrified. Reckon she could have been trying to say something like 'Madam, steal money.' Makes sense."

"It sure does," the young constable responded, kicking the seabag away and coming erect as Karpis groaned his defeat and made a useless attempt to grab at the colorful and distinctive tin box the man had found.

The Karpis howled in reaction to a fresh wave of agony as his bullet-shattered knee crashed against the pier.

The policeman holstered his gun and held the box in the crook of an arm as he twisted off the lid. He grinned and nodded as he looked up, across the writhing form of the injured man toward the impassive Steele.

"Looks to be about five thousand, mister," he revealed, and raised the open box close to his face. He sniffed at it. "Plus a gun that's been fired not too long ago. Things'll have to be checked out officially, but I figure you're off the hook."

"In more ways than one," Steele murmured as he stooped to pick up the empty rifle and glanced back along the pier and across the dock at the warehouses.

"What's that?" the policeman asked as he closed the lid of the box.

"Just thinking aloud," the Virginian answered, rubbing a gloved hand over the bristles on his jaw as he canted the Colt Hartford to his shoulder. "Right now I've got . . .

. . . *nothing more to say.*"*

---

* Until he has to talk and fight his way out of new troubles in the next Adam Steele story.

EDGE

BY
George G. Gilman

More bestselling western adventure from Pinnacle, America's #1 series publisher. Over 6 million copies of EDGE in print!

GET ACQUAINTED!
THREE BESTSELLING ACTION/ADVENTURE SERIES FROM PINNACLE BOOKS